Praise for *The Private War of William Styron*

"Mary Wakefield Buxton has revealed the true essence of the life of Pulitzer Prize-winning author William Styron in her new book, *The Private War of William Styron*. Because of Buxton's close relationship to Styron, she uncovers truths we might otherwise never have known."

— Tom Hardin, editor, *Southside Sentinel*

"Fans and scholars of the work of Pulitzer Prize-winner William Styron will find intensity and insight in this fictional approach to the author's art and anguish. 'Could a woman writer dare to get into the mind of a male writer? Could a woman tell a man's story?' Buxton asks. Her answer: yes, she can."

— Bill Ruehlmann, book reviewer, the *Virginian Pilot* and Norfolk *Ledger Star*

"Mary Wakefield Buxton describes perfectly in her book *The Private War of William Styron* the universal struggle of that rare, non-conforming and artistic soul who must insist on following his or her own path in life, totally disregarding flak from the common herd along the way. A magnificent read from a gifted writer."

— John Selby Spong, former rector of St. Paul's Episcopal Church, Richmond Virginia, and author of *The Fourth Gospel: Tales of a Jewish Mystic*

"Mary Wakefield Buxton writes with a passion and knowledge of Bill Styron's life that cannot be surpassed."

— Larry Chowning, author of *Barcat Skipper* and staff reporter, *Southside Sentinel*

"[Buxton] provides a mission as sentry, alert to the inconsistencies, prejudices, and paradoxes in life. No one, as poet Wordsworth said of a host of daffodils, could be but gay in such jocund company."

— Guy Friddel, *Richmond News Leader*, Norfolk *Ledger Star*

More Praise for Mary Wakefield Buxton

"This writer pokes fun and criticism at southern genteel . . . [she is] the insightful and purposeful scribbler of an enlightened pen."
— Werner Saemmler Hindriches, Fredericksburg citiLimits

"I call her iconoclastic. She writes strong stuff."
— Parke Rouse, the *Daily Press*

"William Styron once said, 'But of all the schools I attended . . . only Christchurch ever commanded something more than mere respect—which is to say, my true and abiding affection.' Mary Buxton masterfully brings to life the early years of one of Christchurch School's favorite sons and most distinguished alumni. *The Private War of William Styron* adds new research and a fresh perspective to understanding this complicated genius."
— John E. "JEB" Byers, headmaster, Christchurch School

Also by Mary Wakefield Buxton

Rappahannock River Journeys
Help! I'm Being Held Captive in Virginia!
Return to the Rappahannock
To Love a Virginian
Sunrise on the Rappahannock
The Great Rappahannock River Race
One Woman's Opinion: The Story of a Small Town Writer
Bringing in the Wood: The Way it Was at Chesapeake Corporation
Bound for Urbanna
Middlesex Memories: Our Place and Our Times
Love Stories: People and Places in Middlesex County

The Private War of William Styron

The Private War of William Styron

a novel

By Mary Wakefield Buxton

Mary W Buxton

❀ *Brandylane*

Printed in the United States
ISBN: 978-1-9399300-1-9
Library of Congress Control Number: 2014940667

Cover photo of William Styron provided courtesy of Christchurch School, Middlesex County, Virginia

Back cover wedding photo of Elizabeth Buxton Styron (circa 1940) provided courtesy of Joseph T. Buxton III

Published by

🌸 *Brandylane* Publishers, Inc.
WWW.BRANDYLANEPUBLISHERS.COM

For Bill and Elizabeth

ACKNOWLEDGEMENTS

I wish to thank my husband, Joseph T. "Chip" Buxton III for his encouragement as I wrote this book and for providing me the photograph of his Aunt Elizabeth Buxton Styron on her wedding day, Rose Styron for her ongoing interest in my project, and Christchurch School in Middlesex County, Virginia, which provided me with the photo of young Bill Styron as a student in his senior year. I could not have finished the book without the dedicated help of my cousin, Molly Wakefield Milner, who spent over a year editing every word. It would not have been published without Robert Pruett of Brandylane Publishers, who took an interest in preserving a bit of Virginia literary history. And finally, I appreciate such patient and detailed final editing by Erin Harpst. Thank you, all.

December 19, 1990

Dear Mary,

I was very taken by your letter and its analysis of the Buxton Family and its syndrome, or curse, or whatever it may be . . .

Faithfully,
Bill

July 9, 2002

Dear Mary,

I thought your piece in the [*Southside*] *Sentinel* was extremely good—perceptive and very well written (so many interviews I've had are filled with errors) and you did a great job of capturing the feeling of our down and out struggling school at the end of the Depression. Also, you were justly tough but fair-minded about Elizabeth. All in all beautifully done . . .

Love,
Bill

Author's Note

This is a work of art, mostly fiction, created from my own mad fantasies and struggles as a writer and based on characters I knew well, many of whom are now passed away. It is my way of explaining for posterity what I believe was the source of the life-long depression suffered by one of the greatest writers of our time, William Styron.

CHAPTER 1

The Funeral

I t was here, in the fall of 1940, that Father had married her. In this very
same church.

St. Paul's Episcopal Church was exactly as it had been then. Nothing
had changed. It was as if time had not passed in this corner of the world and
everything had stood still. He had sat in this very pew, at fifteen years old.

Now it was the summer of 1969, and he was back for his stepmother's
funeral. The woman is dead, he remembered, and the thought washed
through his brain like water suddenly doused on fire. But—how strange—he
still felt her presence. She had left plans for every detail of her funeral: the
hymns to be sung, the rector chosen to give the eulogy, the pews to which all
were duly assigned, the pallbearers, the flowers, even the linen that was spread
out to receive her as she lay regally within her coffin next to the altar. As a last
command, she might have ordered that her stepson, Billy, be made to feel as
guilty as possible.

"Zip up your pants, Billy! Sit up straight in the pew, Billy!"

God! He could still hear her voice. Even now, all these years later, he
could feel his innards recoil at her obsession for neatness and detail. She ran
her own funeral as if she were still with them, as if she were still the director of
the nursing school in her father's hospital, in a milieu where no imperfection
was allowed to exist.

He felt the impact of his desperate thoughts as they raced from his brain
to every other organ, from artery to vein and cell to pore, like circuits gone
mad, inundating his entire body with an electric charge. I am here only for

Father, he repeated over and over to himself like some comforting mantra, each soothing word delivered deep into his brain, in hopes of calming himself. But how could he possibly survive the weekend?

His father, whose name he carried, sat on one side of him, still handsome in his dark suit and silver tie, even though hunched over in the pew, his thick head of hair as white as snow. He had seen two women to their graves in his lifetime, first Bill's mother and now Elizabeth, two wives who had suffered the same painful deaths of cancer. Father had lived to bury them both, faithful servant to the end. Oh, noble man!

Organ music filled the church, the chords swelling along with the throngs of those who had come to pay their last respects: family, friends, and the official grievers. Every community had this ilk—the sort who made it their profession to attend all important funerals and parties afterwards. Then there were the usual doctors, nurses, representatives from the best Tidewater society, and, of course, always the curious, for the Buxton family had its own special following, and they were true and loyal to Elizabeth right down to the last man. The natives always stuck together, thick and steamy as crab chowder in a mug.

The first pews were reserved for the immediate family: Russell Buxton, known by the nurses as "Dr. Russell" to differentiate the son from his father, "Dr. Joseph," now deceased, who had built the first hospital on the peninsula in 1906; Russell's second wife, Virginia; and on the other side of Russell, his crippled sister, Helen, who wore a wooden leg after suffering a heinous accident as a young girl when a trolley ran over her in front of the hospital. Behind that group sat another brother, John, a retired Navy captain who graduated from Annapolis and in World War II had gone on to command a warship that had been hit by a German U-boat torpedo; nevertheless, he'd managed to bring his ship back to Norfolk. Beside him sat his wife, Alice, who could still send ripples through the old guard of the family. They had never approved of a Catholic becoming one of the clan. To round it off were Russell's three sons, Chip, Buck, and Luke, with their wives and young children, and a sprinkling of other relatives including a cousin, the judge, and his family.

Bill's wife, Rose, sat on the other side of him, wearing a splendid hat. She had found it in Elizabeth's closet before the funeral, amongst a full array of round hatboxes, each hat packed fastidiously in tissue by those determined, long and fluttering fingers. It was as if Elizabeth had known that Rose would not come from Bill and Rose's home in Connecticut properly prepared to attend a church funeral in the South; that is, without the hat, gloves, and black dress deemed proper for a funeral by the judgmental, ever-watching Southern army.

Bill recalled the earlier scene at the house before they had left for the church. Oh, but there had been an outburst of laughter. Wondrous, glorious laughter! It had rung through the house like the sudden outbreak of chiming cathedral bells and left the group stunned. Rose and Mary, Chip's wife, had found each other in that dreary house, and, each being of a naturally merry disposition which not even a funeral could eradicate, became immediate friends through the simple discovery of the somewhat hilarious news that neither owned a hat to wear to the funeral. They had dashed up the stairs together to Elizabeth's bedroom in search of something appropriate.

Bill followed them up the stairs, a desperate man, and watched as they gaily tore through the ample collection of hatboxes. Oh, which hat would it be? A Mary Poppins straw hat with long black streamer for Mary? A velvet cloche for Rose? A paisley turban? A pillbox special à la Jackie Kennedy? A flowered Easter bonnet? A black felt fedora adorned with a surprising feather?

How that dreadful house, filled with its oiled and creaking antique furniture and silver reflecting the austere faces of the past, had been filled with shrieks of feminine laughter as each hat was tried on and paraded in front of mirrors. The sound of happy laughter had come to him, unexpected as the notes of a Scottish lilt drifting suddenly from a coal mine. The sound had spread from the dismal upstairs front bedroom where Elizabeth had spent her last year of life, slowly dying of cancer in her four-poster maple bed, and could be heard throughout the house.

There hadn't ever been laughter like that emanating from Elizabeth's bedroom, Bill thought, as he sat on the bedroom chaise lounge and watched the show of hats. By God, how he longed for laughter! He was suddenly filled with a giddy feeling of hope. He had taken the glass of whiskey in his hand and swallowed what remained of it in one long, comforting gulp. Writer comes home to bury stepmother, he thought. Writer cringes in former bedroom of stepmother. He hears laughter and feels for the first time that he might just survive this egregious level of inferno, the one Dante must certainly have reserved for the burial of stepmothers.

I am here only for Father, he reminded himself once again.

Bill shifted in the hard wooden pew to gain relief from a sudden pain in his lower back, as thoughts continued to race through his brain. That he had returned for her funeral so many years after he had left—now a well-known writer who had won the Pulitzer Prize for *Sophie's Choice*—offered meager consolation. Elizabeth never thought much of me as a writer, he remembered. Not that it mattered one iota to him what she thought about him or anything else.

In a terrifyingly Proustian flashback popped forth from some deep pocket in his brain, she suddenly reappeared before him in full regalia, rising up from her coffin, like some horrifying specter, rolling her pale blue eyes in that face of deathly white pallor, with its skin that had ever shied away from the sun. "Watch your language, Billy!" she snapped at him in front of the entire congregation.

"Billy thinks he's a writer," her shrill voice continued, rising to include the entire church congregation. She delivered her usual judgment du jour, harshly, like a scratchy tune played on an old Victrola: "Billy thinks he's a writer." She had repeated that same phrase again and again and again to her innumerable friends and relations all those long years until he had almost lost his mind—throughout his youth, his young adulthood, even after his books were being published, those damnable words—all the while rolling her eyes to such an extreme that he thought they would surely recede into the cathedral of her brain.

"But of course, I was a writer, you damned fool woman," he mouthed under his breath. He could still feel the fury rising within him. But, then, in the end, he knew the terrifying truth: that every writer must hoist his own flag, scream over the universal familial doubts, slay the ridicule and protests and shout to all the world, "I am a writer! Damn you all to hell!"

After the merry episode of the hats, he had hunkered down and thought all these black dog thoughts in a straight-backed chair in the corner of the breakfast nook just off the kitchen, the same chair where he had sat most miserably at so many breakfasts in years past. It was Chip's new wife, Mary, still in her twenties and just back from her husband's military service in Japan, who had approached him. She had purposely sought him out in the pre-funeral throng gathered at the house. A young woman from Ohio, recently married into the family, she still had a stunned look on her face. She had moved to a chair beside him and introduced herself, and he had peeked up at her and seen that she still had her straw hat on her head and that her blonde curls popped out of the straw like chicks escaping their nest. He could tell immediately that she was innocent of the ways of the South by her rounded eyes, like two shiny buckeyes just fallen from a tree, staring in wonder at everything she saw. She even had a freckled nose, as one might suspect someone from Ohio to have, someone who cared not a fig if she were caught in the sunshine without a hat. She laughed a lot, and he liked her for it. He knew instantly that she revered him because he was a writer; one learns over time to recognize such responses in so-called fans. So he began to talk—ramble on and on, really. Bill was well into his balm, "Uncle Jack," and was rapidly moving into that delicious zone where one can go if necessary. It was a bit like being wing on wing on the sea, in no condition to talk, but ever so willing to babble about any topic to any sympathetic ears he could find.

And why not? He was hiding from the vacuous masses of people that had come to the house before the funeral, Elizabeth's string of prominent friends whom his father so adored. His father's only weakness of character was in liking her society too much: her hundreds of nurse graduates; her brother, Dr. Russell, the surgeon who practiced in his late father's profession, who carried on the family duty, name and tradition; the ladies of the church; and the doting, unctuous neighbors whispering throughout the rooms, "Where's Billy?" and craning their necks in their search. Bill didn't want to see any of them. They were why he had finally left Virginia so many years ago, to escape Elizabeth and the whole horrid lot of her revering throng.

He remembered how he had talked to Mary about his first book, *Lie Down in Darkness*, the book that had so boldly described his native home in Tidewater, Virginia, as a relic of a decayed Southern society, the book that had launched his career as a writer. He'd told her, in broken whiskey-induced fragments of sentences that came in no specific sequence, how odd it was, how the book had seemingly spilled out of him like water from a faucet suddenly turned on, and the streams had gushed forth over that hideous stone, moss, and mishmash of weeds, filling the trays of archaic pots, flooding the terrace and last year's dead flower bed, pooling along the dank and musty foundations of the house.

Darkness, those wretched little people, their addiction to judgment and puritanical hypocrisy, their inability to forgive the scores of mean and petty incidents that had occurred throughout their lives—oh, he had nailed them good.

He'd been in his twenties and living in New York when he wrote that first novel. It had aged him, that book, so filled with rage and written under the feverish strain of the hepatitis that had weakened him that year, the passion for telling his story exploding out of his brain and connecting with his pen as it scrawled across the yellow legal pad he balanced on his lap. The words flowed forth from him with such force that after them, he had never been the same.

But he had captured the Virginians. He had done that. He had chased them like butterflies and netted them one by one and pinned them to a board, displayed their fancy, transparent wings spread miserably and forever in the cold air of truth for all to see. Oh God, he had done that!

The sudden cessation of the organ prelude interrupted his thoughts of the past. The priest rose from his throne next to God and raised his hand to signal the beginning of the opening hymn: "A Mighty Fortress Is Our God!" It was exactly the hymn he had expected from Elizabeth. She would have us all march off to do battle against the Devil. He sang the vile words only because he was seated next to his father. He could feel the tremor in the poor man's body. How he had suffered! And yes, of course he would sing the bloody hymn—if only to please him. But he was thirsty. So thirsty. He wished they served bourbon for communion in the Episcopal Church.

At the end of the hymn, the rector, dressed in white, stood like an archangel before his troops and approached a podium of rich paneled wood that reeked of respect. The carved eagle at the lectern glared down at the congregation with typically furious Episcopalian expression, wings unsheathed for flight, talons ready to strike, as if the parishioners themselves were its desired prey. If he had believed in God, which he most emphatically did not—if he had owned in his soul any inkling of hope that such a force even existed—would he ever have allowed such a frightful symbol to be placed before him? Never!

Rose nudged him in a way that vanquished his swirling, dark thoughts. She had that power over him. She pointed to a prayer to be recited in unison from a well-thumbed page in the prayer book. He read the words in rote fashion, as if they were multiplication tables recited to a fourth grade teacher, if for no other reason than to please his poor, duped father.

"O God of grace and glory, we remember before you this day our sister Elizabeth. We thank you for giving her to us, her family and friends, to know and to love as a companion on our earthly pilgrimage . . . " he mumbled in unison with the congregation.

At last, the priest motioned for them to sit down, and the entire congregation settled back into the unforgiving and creaking wooden pews.

There was the usual rustling of paraphernalia, the banging of kneeling platforms being placed upright—and the coughing. My God! Does everyone in this church have a cold? Bill wondered. Never had he heard so much coughing.

His thoughts returned to his father. He was a North Carolinian and Presbyterian by birth and ancestry but had been quickly swallowed by the more powerful Virginia Episcopalians, as so many people who moved to the area were. Virginians always prevail in the end. All resisting voices fade under their spell, he thought. His father had endured the long days and nights and the unceasing orders, watching the life ebb out of a woman he so deeply revered. Elizabeth's death, like his mother's, had been a slow death. It was like a rerun of a nightmarish film. How terrible that his father had experienced it twice. And yet for the son, who now lived so far away in the north, the loss of his stepmother had inspired an emotion that was precisely opposite of the sharp grief he had experienced from his own mother's death so long ago.

" . . . In your boundless compassion, console us who mourn. Give us faith to see in death the gate of eternal life; so that in quiet confidence we may continue our course on earth, until, by your call, we are reunited with those who have gone before; through Jesus Christ our Lord. Amen."

"Stop crying!" Dr. Buxton barked out the sudden stern command to his sister, Helen, in the first pew. His voice carried like an echo of gunshot through the church, as if to put all mourners on notice that tears would not be tolerated. Not in this family. His words could have been spoken by Elizabeth herself, for the brother and sister had held the same stern values. They had always seen public displays of grief as a sign of character weakness. Mankind was meant to carry its heartbreak in life with a firm chin and stoic heart. It was a matter of class. Let the common herd cry into their hankies—but not this family. The crippled youngest sister had relied on Elizabeth throughout her life for most everything. Now she was failing Elizabeth at her funeral service by bringing embarrassment to the family. Pathetic woman. She could not stop her weeping in public.

Bill's thoughts returned to the night that Elizabeth had finally recognized him as a writer. How the memory still thrilled him: that flashback to the past and the pure magnificence of it all. No one could have planned it better. After he had won the Pulitzer Prize, Father had been sitting in the library listening to the news on TV when Walter Cronkite announced his name: "William Styron, born in Newport News, Virginia, has just won the Pulitzer Prize for Literature." Father had leapt from his chair and rushed to the kitchen, where Elizabeth stood paring apples at the sink, and he had grabbed her by the waist and spun her around and around the room, laughing and crying all at the same time. "I guess now you'll have to agree that Billy is a writer!" he had shouted over and over again. That story was told again and again within the family—and the entire community—how Elizabeth, at long last, had reluctantly put down her knife and agreed with Father that Billy really was a writer, after all those many years. Hearing this account had been like a cool salve spread on a hot and festering wound.

"She was the epitome, all those many years, of the Buxton Hospital nurse, ever on duty, ever alert to detail, the bulwark of the family's ongoing commitment to providing the best medical health services to the peninsula . . ." spoke a staff doctor in eulogy. Dr. Russell rose to say a few words in tribute to his sister, who had dedicated her life to the hospital and the nursing school. He was followed by the priest, who had adored her, for who had always taken charge of the annual downtown Lenten lunches? And then came more hymns and prayers, falling into each other in a union of reverent mumbled words.

The service ended in one glorious burst of song, the organ driving the musical notes, if not the audience, to the heights of heaven, the congregation swelling with emotion and words. Rose again touched her husband at the base of his elbow, and he stood up, turned, and blindly followed his father as they were escorted from the pew. They were joined by Elizabeth's family: the doctor, the captain, the Catholic wife, the lawyer, his freckled wife from Ohio, the judge—a veritable swarm of them: cousins, nieces, nephews, brothers, sisters, the cripple with her wooden leg and tear-streaked face; the entire clan, all in one moving blur. They gathered together behind the flowered coffin and bowed their heads in shared grief, following her all the way down that red-carpeted aisle, precious jewels glowing in the windows, the well-shod feet stepping in and out of the spilled rubies strewn across the carpet, with every neck crooked, every jaundiced, narrow eye aimed at them. They got into the limousines and drove to the country club, to the next round of drinks; they made it to the bar, clutched their drinks, smiled, nodded, remembered fond stories, shook hands, pressed shoulder to shoulder into their task, and bolted their bourbon. With a frozen look pasted on his face, Bill watched as they all did their duty; by God, they did their duty, Virginia style. And Bill knew, in the deepest recesses of his heart, that she would have been proud of the perfect service that had been held in her honor, even though her stepson occupied the same pew that he had when he'd witnessed her marriage to his father in 1940, and was feeling anew the same fury she'd instilled in him then. And he knew that nothing had changed.

CHAPTER 2

The Night Before the Funeral

Rose and Bill had come to Newport News the evening before the funeral, arriving at Elizabeth's old white frame house on Chesapeake Avenue overlooking the Hampton Roads waterway where he and his father had moved after his father's remarriage. The house was located conveniently near her father's hospital and the nursing school where she had served as director. She could easily walk to and from her work, and it was only a short drive across town to his father's office at the shipyard.

It was miserable today, as it was then, the usual Tidewater summer fare: fearsomely hot and humid. Across Chesapeake Avenue, the busy street that ran along the shore and separated the house from the river, steam rose off the water. It was the same stifling, non-air-conditioned heat he remembered from that first summer he spent in that house when he would lie in a pool of sweat in bed each night in the back bedroom, praying for a whiff of cool air. He could hear the same call of a mockingbird that he remembered so well from childhood, along with the distant cry of gulls ever savaging the shore, and the gentle hoot of an owl. He could smell the same mix of seaweed and mud at low tide and see the same twinkling lights as he looked out the window. But how rapidly such senses brought back the horror of that first summer, when he was a fifteen-year-old boy.

He now lay on the bed where his father had slept for so many years, where he was available for Elizabeth's call from her sickbed on the other side of the archway, which had been cut between the two front bedrooms. The twilight lent a slight breeze from the mouth of the James River, and he heard the faint swish of pale curtains rustling against the windowsill. A pair of enamored cardinals had made an early evening connection just outside in the old magnolia tree that lightly brushed against the front windows. He could hear the last notes of their love song in the thickening dusk.

Fully dressed, he sprawled, exhausted, across his father's four-poster bed, the one that matched her bed in the adjoining room with the exact same type of horsehair mattress. He could smell her in the next room, as if she were still alive, that faint whiff of Yardley's Old English Lavender with which she doused herself each morning and which lasted all day long . . . that sickening sweetness that followed her whenever she entered the room. Fragrance lasts on certain people even long after death.

In spite of the starched and ironed sheets, he could feel the sharp stab of horsehair in his back. Horsehair! He and Rose had given her these very mattresses when they had asked her once what she wanted for Christmas. She had responded that she ardently wished for a set of old-fashioned, handmade horsehair mattresses, like what she had slept on as a girl in the big house farther down the avenue. They had laughed out loud at the eccentric request and then realized that she was quite serious, Elizabeth being a woman to seldom make a joke. Rose had finally located a company that could make them to order and had the twin mattresses shipped to her for Christmas. She had been delighted.

His eyes came to rest on the maple dressing table in her part of the adjoining bedroom. His gaze fell to a hairbrush still laced with her grey hair, as if she had just brushed before retiring for the night. He shivered.

Rose was downstairs talking with members of the family who were still hanging on to their blessed moment of shared grief with Father. Sentence fragments came floating up the staircase and into the bedroom: She was such a dedicated woman . . . One could always count on Elizabeth . . . They don't make that kind of woman anymore—bits of flotsam and jetsam loosed upon the sea. The voices were low and measured, as if those who spoke were afraid of disturbing somebody, as if she were still upstairs and dying in the front bedroom. Their words played on his brain like the notes of a bass fiddle. Oh, that he could fall asleep and leave this wretched world with all its painful memories behind!

Bill propped up his head with a pillow so that he could see out the window. In the deepening dusk, he could see the lights of Norfolk across the water. Just like when he was a boy, warships were berthed at the U.S. naval base, and this weekend the SS *United States*, lit up in her own private galaxy, rested at a commercial dock. She had arrived earlier in the day, majestically entering Hampton Roads from New York City; they had seen her approach as they landed at Patrick Henry Airport. Since the captain knew Elizabeth, he had tooted a salute to her, as was his custom, not knowing she received this greeting from her coffin.

Bill's eyes swept from the distant lights to the bedroom. It was perfect, as was her style, and he felt the chill of its perfection from behind the seclusion of his half-closed eyelids. The room had been conscientiously, methodically assembled with just the right accessories, antiques from her earlier home at the old grandiose stone mansion down the avenue mixed in with all the right accessories of time and place, so typical in the South. Things must match; colors must harmonize; nothing should jolt the senses. There were doilies tatted by delicate spinster aunts, crystal vases passed down from earlier generations, and linens, embroidered by believing fingers and kept starched, bleached, and ironed by the faithful Veala, the long-serving and loyal family maid. All were set off by a soft green carpet against an eggshell wall—shades of color no doubt deemed perfectly correct for Tidewater homes in 1969.

Bits and pieces of china graced the dresser and tables. They came from the hospital, as did the bud vase, which had once held a single bright red rose, sprigs of azalea, or gardenia, and which had been placed on a tray at breakfast or afternoon tea in order to cheer a discouraged heart. The family-owned hospital always made that extra effort.

Portraits of Elizabeth's father and mother, the much-idolized and revered founders of the hospital and nursing school, hung on the wall. They looked down at him quizzically, almost curiously, as he sprawled across the bed, as if they wondered what he was doing in their daughter's home, and like their daughter, also wondered whether he really was a writer. He had never known them, since they had both passed on before his father's fateful marriage, but he certainly knew of their sterling reputations. Father never stopped talking of the sacred pair, as if they were gods. The city had been so grateful for their work in the field of health that it named the avenue leading to the hospital from downtown Newport News after the family.

The hospital was run with as much perfection as could ever be expected or generated from mere humans. After her mother retired from her work as director of the Buxton Nursing School, Elizabeth had taken her place supervising this perfection. She stood faithfully on duty along with her brother, Dr. Russell, until 1953. At that time, the hospital had been sold to the Bernadine Sisters, a Catholic order from Philadelphia. The denomination of the sisters had not gone unnoticed by the local army of those all too willing to pass judgment on all things.

This was a family that knew that the business of life and death was not to be taken lightly. They were obsessed with developing a staff that would create the best hospital anywhere. Germs were a constant threat—a scalpel improperly sanitized, a candy wrapper left at the nurses' station, an unflushed toilet, a cigarette butt thrown carelessly, or a wet towel on the floor could precipitate serious infections. Such signs pointed to slovenly behavior and were never tolerated.

Elizabeth had recalled many times to him how her father had arrived unannounced one day at the nurses' private quarters in the early years of the nursing school. The ladies had quieted instantly as the great man swept into their presence. He had stopped and glanced disapprovingly at an offending drawer that had been left ajar by some frivolous hand. He moved toward it and thrust it open to unveil some nurse's private trove of chocolate. With a howl of rage, he yanked out the drawer and spilled the contents across the floor. "Clean this up at once!" he ordered and then left as swiftly as he'd come, his brisk footsteps fading across the tile into a final slammed door at the end of the corridor. It had been her favorite "Papa" story.

Not just candy was prohibited, but also the bouts of giggling or the sharing of daily gossip that one might expect from young women during off-hours or breaks. That sort of behavior was looked upon with strong disapproval. Such activities suggested merriment or foolishness, and this might be indicative of someone shirking her duty. It was unheard of to find nurses or any other staff grouped together in the corridors, casually sipping mugs of coffee, trading off-color jokes with the remains of donut frosting on their lips and hands, laughing, or flirting with a male patient or orderly.

This was the atmosphere in which Elizabeth had been raised and had practiced her profession. Bill had not fully understood her particular background of discipline and drive for perfection in that first year after she had married his father. It took him many more years to gain such insight. The unfortunate reality was that he had become a part of her mission. He was her "most fortunate" stepson—destined to become the next doctor in the family.

CHAPTER 3

Interview with the Headmaster

Bill was tired. He needed sleep. He would let Rose handle the family visits downstairs and have a short nap. He could feel his body pressing deeper into the horsehair mattress and his eyelids sinking over his eyes. Would he sleep now, perchance to dream?

The darkness came over him like an encroaching curtain. Perhaps he himself had died along with Elizabeth. She was somewhere in her coffin, but he could feel himself floating upward in some undefined space made up of black matter. As he went off to distant shores, a great sadness fell over him.

He knew that Elizabeth's influence on his father had been the cause of his going to boarding school. Of course he knew it. At the age of fifteen, he had visited Christchurch School for the first time with his father and Elizabeth. She had been there to make sure the headmaster knew of the impending marriage, and to gently illustrate to the headmaster who was going to be the new boss in the family—and who, therefore, had to be pleased.

Bill was a thin and awkward boy then, skinny for his height but already in possession of a well-cut, handsome face, with light sandy hair, pale blue eyes, and fair skin that bespoke his English genes—the kind of looks that would one day catch the eye of many an admiring woman.

He already had a dreamy look on his young face, as if he weren't quite a part of this world—or, if he were in the present, a suggestion that there was at least a part of him that might be somewhere else. Perhaps this expression hinted that one day he would become a writer, for out of the young dreamers in this world eventually emerge the "artistes."

So here he was, a boy who had just lost his mother, a boy who preferred to spend his days with his own thoughts rather than be bothered with the English, Latin, algebra, science, or history that had to be mastered so that he could go to college.

With him that fateful day were his father and, at his father's side, Elizabeth, tall and dignified as usual, dressed in a grey suit, matching hat, gloves, and pocketbook. A snatch of lace grew from her throat, perhaps to prove she was a woman. Her heels were thick, as if she planned on leading a troop of Girl Scouts through a field to gather wildflower specimens.

Elizabeth had cared for Bill's father in the hospital when he was so depressed after his wife died. She had fluttered and doted over his every need as he lay helplessly in his hospital bed. Bill supposed she had realized her opportunity now that he was a widower, and she wasted no time moving in. They had begun to date when he was back home again in Hilton Village, Newport News, the same year.

And now they were planning to get rid of him, or so it seemed to the boy. They said he must be sent away to school to be inspired to study—but he always knew, deep down, that they really did it to be done with him, so that they could get on with their own selfish lives.

"Billy has trouble following rules and concentrating on his studies," Elizabeth had told his father. "He wants to run wild with his pack of friends like wolves in the night and drink, smoke, and get into trouble." And Father had listened to her.

Everything Billy had known was about to come to an abrupt end. He had lost his mother, moved to a new home and neighborhood, and was disconnected forever from old friends. A new mother now, a stepmother, was sending him away to a new school. There were conversations: he had to have a good education, he had to make something of himself, become a doctor or a lawyer, some respectable profession—perhaps be like Father, an engineer, and spend a lifetime, as Father had, locked up in an office at the shipyard.

But didn't he already spend days and nights scribbling snatches of stories, conversations, events, weaving feelings and words into the mystery of a good tale? Didn't he already take in the world around him with all of his young senses in first gear? He was young, but hadn't he already suffered immeasurable pain? Didn't they understand that he wanted to know truth, that he craved something genuine in this world, but most of all, that he wanted to know real people?

Father and Elizabeth approached the headmaster's office and went up the steps and through the door as if they were happy. He followed them with little interest, letting his eyes linger on the rolling green lawn that sloped down in a gentle curve to the river and imagining a sailing trip far out to the bay.

Boys were playing football on the field, and he could hear their voices calling from across the green. There was a sudden shout from the gym, and a few boys who had gathered under a tree stopped their conversation and watched intently as young Billy walked up the steps behind the two adults.

"Tuck in your shirttail, Billy," Elizabeth hissed. God, how that woman hissed! Like a serpent in the back garden! What gave her the right to instruct him as to how to dress? He felt the prick of her words like an ice pick at his insides.

They sat in the lobby on a trio of pale green brocade Queen Anne chairs with backs so high and straight that a young man who tended to slouch was forced to sit with perfect posture. A kind-looking woman slipped through the double doors and announced to Headmaster Smith, whom Billy would come to love, that his Newport News appointment had arrived.

It was hot. By God, it was hot! A ceiling fan made lazy turns above but did little to cool the room. The sweat dripped down Billy's neck and back and left his shirt and the waist of his slacks drenched. He wiggled uncomfortably in his chair, pulling at his blazer. He could barely breathe in the close air.

Father was called in first for a private meeting with the headmaster that lasted a long time. Billy sat stiffly as Elizabeth watched over him with the same interest she might have shown a foreign insect she'd found on her best shrub. He ignored her probing blue eyes that took all things in. Did she suspect he might suddenly bolt for the fields, a wild thing that would disappear like a rabbit in the brush, to live a life forever on the loose, never to be seen in civilization again? He hovered over a magazine and pretended to read. How she smiled faintly as she watched his every move, as if to show pride that he was actually her son! Those pale blue eyes, those thick glasses that magnified their size. She dabbed her glistening forehead with a lace handkerchief and he could smell the cloying whiff of Yardley's Old English Lavender cologne in the stifling air. Immediately, nausea swept over him. He wanted to cry out to the muffled voices from within the inner office door and the woman who sat at her desk, briskly typing on a black typewriter.

"Come in, Billy," Headmaster Smith finally announced, opening the double doors and extending his hand. He looked to be a friendly man of short height and trim body, with ruddy cheeks and a full head of sandy-colored hair. His neck was bright red and tightly laced with a shirt and school tie, and he looked as if he had stood out in the bright sun on too many soccer fields, endlessly cheering on the boys. "Your father and I were just discussing some of the difficult changes you have had to adjust to in your life."

They shook hands. Billy mumbled a few polite words he had memorized to carry him through any contact with adults, then slipped helplessly into a chair opposite his father.

"I understand your father will be married soon, Billy," Headmaster Smith continued, returning to his red leather chair. "And to an exceedingly fine woman, a prominent leader in her community, I understand. Your father is very proud and happy to become her husband. It is a good time for you to join us at Christchurch," he added with a pleasant smile. Billy winced at the words, feeling like a fish suddenly caught by the barb of a hook and jerked up from the sea.

Father was going to be married! Of course, he had been told about Father's plan to wed that woman, but it was something he had immediately rejected as preposterous. Father loved my mother! How could he marry another woman? Let alone that monster of a woman!

Billy stared straight ahead, not looking at anyone, and felt the hot swell of tears wanting to escape from behind his eyes. He blinked hard in the bright lights to hold them back. He could feel his heart pounding in his chest and a wretched churning deep in his gut.

"I love Elizabeth, son," Father said in a soft tone that changed Billy's shock to disgust. He felt as if he might be sick. That woman! Love! All eyes were on the young boy, and he somehow knew that he had to be strong. Headmaster Smith must never see him weep or keel over on his oriental rug in desperate throes of vomiting.

Billy's concern over what the headmaster thought of him quickly passed, and he was suddenly filled with a sensation of rage. He leapt to his feet, as if charged with electricity.

"How could you love that woman?" he shouted at his father. The idea seemed as preposterous to him as someone loving a rock. He felt momentarily wild, like some poor, tortured beast that had been poked by a sharp stick and had finally broken its chains and attacked its tormentor. His suffering had gone on so long in silence. What a relief it was that at last it was out in the open for his father to see.

His passion spent, he sat down again, feeling exorcised, if a bit foolish. There was a long silence, as the two men seemed to struggle with pangs of embarrassment. The headmaster looked down, pretending to examine several papers on his desk.

"You are too young to understand loneliness, son," Father finally said.

The headmaster began talking, but Billy heard nothing. Such pat speeches had been issued by headmasters since the founding of the very first boarding school. They were always rife with stock sayings filled with good sense offered up in long, terrifying passages laced with encouraging nods, good will toward man—that sort of rot.

The headmaster continued talking for some time. Billy knew this because he saw the man's lips moving in a synchronized pattern that suggested complete, logical sentences—but he never heard a word.

At last the father and son rejoined that woman. There were hushed bits of conversation as they made their way out to the parking lot, concerning dashed hopes, mainly the unpleasant fact that Billy had not qualified for any ardently hoped for scholarship money, and his father unfortunately would have to pay the full tuition out of his modest engineer's salary from the shipyard.

"You're a most fortunate young man," Elizabeth said, at last turning on her bright smile of victory. Billy already knew well that women had such glorious moments. Life was measured up into bits and pieces of little family battles, and she was a woman who meant to win them.

They walked back to the car to fetch his trunk. "Imagine having to pay your $750 in tuition a year!" she continued. "I hope you will appreciate all the sacrifices we are making for you and that you will study hard and make something of yourself, young man."

Father put his arms around his son and wished him good luck, then turned and left. The treachery was done. Billy watched the green Packard pulling out of the parking lot, Father pausing at the front of the dorm to wave, Elizabeth staring straight ahead. She had the grace, at least, not to wave goodbye to her future stepson, to act as though she cared.

Father had placed Billy's footlocker, packed with all his clothes, on the steps of Bishop Brown dorm. Headmaster Smith, who had followed them out of his office and stood a distance away for their departure, now called a boy to fetch the trunk, put his arm around Billy's shoulder, and led him away to a cubicle in one long open room on the second floor filled with bunks. A new home. He was deposited in the room with his trunk and left to his own resources, as if this happened all the time, fathers coldly leaving their newly motherless sons in some distant dorm to go it alone in life.

Alone in the dorm, he felt that moment's first desperate stab of pain. It happened that fast, Father cutting him out of his life as if he were some unnecessary appendage on his body, like a sixth toe, a third foot, or that obscene wooden leg that that woman's crippled sister, Helen, strapped on her hip each morning, making him cringe in horror every time he saw her.

The insufferable idea that his father no longer needed him had now ferreted a hole deep in his brain, like a rodent in need of a fresh tunnel in moist soil. He threw himself on his cot and wept copiously as the August Tidewater sun sank and at last slipped into the river in the west.

CHAPTER 4

Breakfast at Christchurch

He awoke after that first despairing night in Bishop Brown to the sweet sound of birdsong in rural Virginia. He lay in his bed and let the music of birds fill his sad soul, like medicine sent down from the gods.

Billy had been thrown into a new world of academic brick buildings clumped together in the midst of sky, river, and cornfield. As he listened to the cacophony of tweets, chirps, warbles, and caws, he realized that, for the first time in his life, he did not hear the busy sounds of traffic.

As lovely as the Tidewater morning was, a feeling of extreme loneliness soon passed over him. There is no loneliness like the first morning in prep school, and he had never felt so abandoned in his life. Last year, when Mother had died, he had been out delivering morning newspapers and came back to find her gone, left, vanished—but even then, he hadn't felt as lonely as he did now. Thoughts of his lost mother filled him with emptiness, and he lay helplessly cemented in grief.

Father never talked much about Mother's death, he thought. He guessed his family wasn't the sort to dwell on such things as death. The stiff upper lip, and all that it entailed, was the family modus operandi. But he had known his mother was dying of cancer, and that she was suffering agonizing pain. No one could have kept that knowledge from him at the age of fourteen.

He imagined, on his first morning at Christchurch School, that he had died of the same sort of suffering as his mother had, but that he had awakened in hell. In all Dante's detailed, fastidious layers of imagined tortures for those doomed to eternal punishment, the poet had never imagined a layer as tortuous as Billy's.

He raised his head slowly and looked around the dorm. From his wretched cubicle, he could see sixty similarly damned boys stretched across the large room, sleeping on identical beds in various degrees of disarray. So this was it, he thought. This was where he would spend his last years of high school.

Father meant well. Billy was sure of that. Father's pending marriage to Elizabeth had nothing to do with Billy suddenly being sent away to prep school. Or so he had been told, along with so many other little family lies that one must shoulder throughout one's long life. For when one is young, a life seems long and terrifying, and only when one is older does one see how short life really is.

He knew it was his fault that he had been banished from friends and family. It was true what his father had said. He had not done well at old Morrison School where he had happily spent his earlier years of schooling in Hilton. He had frittered away his time with more than his fair share of Cs and Ds. Father had said he wanted more in life for his son. His father hoped the new school would offer some discipline, help Billy improve his grades, inspire him to pull his life together and make something of himself.

The next boy lay asleep on a rat's nest of a bed nearby. He was sprawled on his back, his ugly mouth agape, his face sporting a load of pimples that raged across a sprinkling of whiskers in his pasty flesh. Even in sleep he appeared to be a maniac, his covers torn and askew and arms flung hopelessly over his head, as if he had given up. An assortment of shoes that appeared to have been rescued from a great puddle of mud peppered the bare wooden floor under his bed. Books, girlie magazines, and dirty underwear, strewn here and there, added to the miserable mess.

Billy rose to his feet, quietly pulled on a shirt and pants, and slid his bare feet into shoes. His cubical was next to the back door of Bishop Brown, so he could easily make his escape into the waiting world of green. Once outside, he stood and took deep breaths of the heady country air and beauty surrounding him. He took it all in, as a drowning man pulled from the sea gasps to fill his lungs with oxygen. The school was set in the midst of fertile farmland and forest. It might have been the Garden of Eden. He had hopes that the rolling, distant fields of soybean and corn, the blue stretch of river, and the dark forests beyond would in some magical way heal him, restore him, and bring him back to life.

He walked across the campus, taking in the chapel, classroom buildings, gymnasium, bell tower, and stately brick and white-columned mansion of Headmaster Smith's family. A lone dog, fresh from a night's sleep, stood at the front porch, and as the boy approached the fence, it walked to the gate to greet him. "Good boy," Billy told the dog, the universal words shared between human and dog forever and ever, while opening the latch and patting his head. Lonely boy met dog and the same old miracle came about that had been happening since the beginning of time; they were instant friends.

The boy and the dog walked together to the Rappahannock River. The dog's wagging tail and the boy's kick of a pinecone as they made their way across the grassy hill seemed to suggest that a long and loving relationship had just begun.

Billy stood and looked at the Rappahannock River for the first time and marveled, as had all who had seen it before him. It was a deep, blue river, unlike the James River, which was shallow, wide, and muddy brown. He remembered his father telling him that the name of the river was a Native American word that meant "serene." He turned to watch the sun come up in the east to a stunning fanfare of pink sky. The river reflected the rosy hues. It was like the first morning of creation. If the cornfields and forests could not heal him, then surely the river and sky would.

Somewhat rejuvenated, with a dog at his side and a pink sky to blind him, he picked up a stick and listlessly threw it into the river. The dog, ecstatic to have a game at last with his new friend, threw himself into the river to retrieve it. Billy saw the enthusiasm of the dog and warmed to the game, which lasted as long as he was willing to heave one more stick. "Good boy!" Billy said each time the stick was dropped at his feet, along with a flurry of water that the retriever delivered faithfully with a wicked shake.

The dog never tired. Billy, who did not himself have a pet, now ached for a dog ever standing by his side—a furry angel sent to help him meet every moment of human emptiness and despair. What more could a boy need in life to fill his empty heart? He reached down and patted the wet, massive head and chest and was immediately filled with an overwhelming sense of love. Casting a furtive look around him to make sure that no one was within sight, he stooped suddenly and threw his arms around the great, sturdy body and wept profusely into the sopping wet fur.

The school bell chimed in the bell tower that stood in the center of the campus, interrupting his melancholy and announcing breakfast. The tower, Headmaster Smith had told him, had been built in the 1920s and dedicated to the memory of a poor boy from school who had drowned in the river. Billy looked up the hill at the bell tower and saw a boy about his age ringing the bell, a task that always went to the best students. He felt that he himself was the drowned boy, come back from the sea.

When the bell stopped tolling, he stood up and wiped the tears from his face. The dog promptly set out for the dining room with wagging tail, as if to encourage Billy to follow; then, when Billy did not immediately do so, he returned to nudge him insistently with his muzzle. "There, there, old boy," the dog might have said to those who had a bent for unusual hearing; "now the crying is done. All the new boys cry when they first come to me. And then it's over, son. Now you will feel better. You'll see. All will be well. Come with me and I will take you up to the dining room to a hot breakfast."

Billy laughed, understanding the imagined message. He decided he would sneak a hot biscuit into his pocket to share with the kind dog after his own breakfast. Suddenly aware of the hunger pang tearing through his stomach, he followed his new pal toward Bishop Brown's basement, where the dining room awaited and wonderful smells emanated from open windows: French toast on the griddle, sizzling bacon, steaming hot biscuits prepared by the colored help to fill the stomachs of lonely, hungry boys. He moved quickly into line and helped himself to a generous serving of scrambled eggs, Virginia ham, and grits dripping in butter, then sat down at an empty table far away from the other boys. As he dug into the food, he realized he was feeling better.

"New boy?" a big, redheaded fellow who had sat down next to him asked, in a deep Southern accent.

"Yeah."

"Where you from?"

"Newport News."

"Cow town. I'm from Atlanta. Capital of the South, old man. What's your name?"

"Bill Styron." Fool, Billy thought. It didn't occur to the other guy to mention his name. Big shot from Atlanta, he supposed. He wasn't going to ask for it either. To heck with him.

"My name's Hudson Lee Butler IV, but they call me 'Poobah,'" the boy said proudly, finally realizing he had not mentioned his name.

Poobah! Billy stared at the fellow. If he could survive in prep school with a name like that, then maybe Billy could, too, even if he had come from a cow town like Newport News.

"Don't you have a nickname?" Poobah asked.

"Nah. Who wants a nickname?"

"What? What? Did you come from some deprived home or something?" Poobah replied. "Everybody here has a nickname. Without a nickname here, you're nobody. Tell you what. I'll call you 'Sty.'"

"Okay," Billy said, feeling a bit embarrassed. He rather liked the nickname "Sty." It had a nice ring to it. He thought it sounded like someone who lived on the streets, understood the world, and knew how to dodge all the pitfalls of life. And it sure beat a nickname like "Poobah."

Sty finished his breakfast and left the dining room to start his first day of classes. Shiloh, the headmaster's faithful dog, with whom he had ventured down to the river, was waiting at the front door for his many charges to pull biscuits out of their pockets one by one and pop them into his waiting mouth. Many of the boys had forgotten their first morning at Christchurch School and the loyal dog that had escorted them to the first breakfast. But not Sty. He delivered his biscuit to his new furry friend just as he knew he should.

Sty smiled. He had a full stomach and a nickname that he liked. It would be a good day, the first day of his new life.

CHAPTER 5

Lunch with Elizabeth

By the way, your father's fiancée, Miss Buxton, is coming today to take you to lunch. This will be a fine opportunity for you and her to have some private time together to get to know each other—just the two of you."

Sty grimaced. Several weeks had passed since the start of school. The headmaster had plunged the dagger of that woman back into his heart just when he had finally forgotten her.

"She's quite a successful person, Sty. You can be very proud of her. I understand she is director of the nursing school at her father's hospital and has held that position for many years since her mother retired. I have heard the school has a reputation up and down the East Coast for producing very fine nurses. It will be quite an honor to have such a distinguished stepmother."

Headmaster Smith looked hopefully at Sty, but he did not respond. "Look, young man, I know this can't be easy for you, your father getting married again and all that. I understand your mother died just last year, but this happens in many families, and learning how to cope with changes is a part of life. We have to make the best of things, old boy. Try to see the bright side of things. Your father must be very lonely now that you are growing up. Why, in another few years you'll be off to college, if you're lucky, that is. The way things are going in Europe just now with the Germans in Poland and France, well, you might even end up in a very nasty war. The important thing to understand is life goes on. We have to turn our attention to other things. Make the best of things, no matter what card is dealt to us in life. You'll be grown up soon and off to live your own life. Your father needs a companion and friend to share his life with as he grows older. We all need that special person . . . "

The headmaster's voice trailed off. Sty was staring hard at a pencil that had been dropped on the sidewalk, and it was obvious that he wasn't listening to one word. Headmaster Smith sighed and patted his ward on the shoulder. "She'll meet you at the chapel steps at noon, Sty. Oh, remember to polish your Sunday shoes and wear your navy school blazer and orange and navy striped tie. This is Christchurch and our boys never leave the campus without wearing their colors and looking their best." He was off.

Sty went off to classes and soon heard the Bell Tower announce the noon hour. He was a few minutes late when he arrived at the chapel. A fancy black Packard convertible that shone like polished coal already waited in the parking lot. That woman sat in the driver's seat.

"Billy," she called through the open window without getting out. "You look like a bum! Go change into a blazer, clean shirt, and tie, and comb your hair. And you also could use a shave! We're going to lunch at the nice hotel dining room in Urbanna, and I want you to look presentable!"

Sty turned back to his dorm, took his time getting himself together, and finally joined her. She did not seem angry that he had kept her waiting at least half an hour.

As he approached the car, she turned a cold eye on him, as if he were a piece of meat that she was debating how to prepare for dinner that night. "Zip up your pants," she ordered and then signaled that he should get into the passenger side and waste no more time. He opened the shiny door, saw the gleaming woodwork panel within, and let out a long, low whistle. The car was brand new and a beauty and he loved it, even though he hated to show her that he was impressed.

She chuckled. "Your father said you would like my fancy car. It was my father's. He just passed away a few months ago. Would you like it if I put the top down?"

"Sure!"

"Let's do it," she responded as she flipped the two switches that held the canvas top firm. Sty got out of the car, neatly folded the collapsed top over the rear ledge, and snapped on the cover that was in the back seat for the finishing touch.

Sty felt flushed with excitement. He had never ridden in such a fine car before, let alone a convertible. He liked it. Driving in it gave him a weird powerful feeling, as if he were floating through air.

Elizabeth drove slowly through the school grounds, taking care with the crowds of boys who were changing classes and drawing closer. As they made their way through the throng, every boy in the school stopped to stare. Sty felt elated, like a king passing through a crowd of milling peasants. He liked the way the other boys stared at him as he sat in the posh Packard.

"Well, you've made an impact on your peers, thanks to my father's car!" Elizabeth said, with that same self-amused chuckle that had already started to grate against the folds of his brain. He didn't want to hear the sound ever again. Perhaps, just perhaps he could learn to tolerate that woman. But never her little private joke kind of laugh.

"I decided to keep Papa's new car for myself, since I'm about to be married and will need a more comfortable car for traveling. It's quite out of character for me to drive such a car, Billy. It's positively shameful!" Again, the self-satisfied chuckle. "But I thought the girls in the nursing school would get a kick out of me, their stern director, keeping such an elegant car. And your father likes the car. He likes nice things. Did you know that about your father?"

He could think of no appropriate response to such a ridiculous remark. "As you know, my father built the first hospital on the peninsula. Although he died last November, just after casting his vote for Mr. Roosevelt, he was a very well-revered and prominent man. You should feel honored to have such a grandfather in your new family!"

Billy stared at the passing fields as they drove toward Urbanna, feeling the splendor of the late summer air spreading through every miserable pore in his stiff body, hearing only the cool roar of the engine beneath the hood and the wind gently passing through his ears. He imagined what it would be like if he had owned such a car and could sit behind the wheel where that woman was now sitting. He knew they would not be moving so slowly if he were the driver of such a car.

"There are certain things that must be said, Billy. You are going to enter a family that has for two generations dedicated their entire lives to delivering the best health care possible to this area. With this legacy, perhaps we are a bit too stern; perhaps we do seem even a bit strange to those of a non-medical background, but health is our mission; nay, it is our total life commitment, Billy. Our patients come first, and family and, yes, even children come second."

Billy did not respond.

"Our family crest bespeaks such tradition," she continued in a voice that droned on and on like an old fan. "It contains a giant bird standing in piety over her nest of fledglings and plucking her own breast with her beak to release blood in order to feed her young. Do you understand such a symbol, son? Our family sacrifices everything for the betterment of our patients. We intend to keep this tradition of health service alive by raising a new generation committed to serving the next generation of citizens of Tidewater, Virginia."

Billy groaned faintly, but she must have heard him, because she stopped her incessant talking. They drove on in silence. The minutes ticked painfully by. "As you know, your father and I are to be wed next month," she suddenly continued, as if she could not wait even one more minute to deal out her black cards. "You will be here at Christchurch School until you graduate, and then off to college. As your new stepmother, I very much want us to have a pleasant relationship. I hope that you feel as I do?"

Billy could not speak. It was as if a jagged bone had wedged itself deep in his throat. He would have spoken, of course; some polite words would have slid out of his lips, thanks to his proper Southern upbringing. As his mother used to remind him, his family might not have had much money, but they had good breeding. She had stressed the importance of being a gentleman and having refined manners no matter what happened in life. That was the real test of good breeding. But now, faced with her, he could not speak.

"Just think, Billy, you could be the next doctor in the family!"

More silence. She sighed, as if finally deciding her words were being wasted on such young and rebellious ears. They approached the low bridge over Urbanna Creek. Now Billy began to show some interest. As they crossed over the bridge, he saw an array of work and pleasure boats tied up along the docks. He could smell the salty, earthy fragrance of low tide and seawater, and he felt an immediate sense of excitement engendered by the presence of the boats. A large, wood-framed skating rink had been built just off the bridge; he could see children entering the building. Beyond that was nestled a clump of buildings: an appliance store that also sold bait, one or two gift and antique stores, and a white-framed Victorian Baptist church.

The Packard slowed to a creep as they made a sharp right to Cross Street. They passed through the village with its gas station, drug store, bank, and the usual small-town grocery and hardware stores.

They turned right again at the Virginia Street intersection and drove down a hill that ran back to Urbanna Creek. An old Colonial brick home sat overlooking the creek on the left and the town library on the right. "That building used to be the old tobacco warehouse, and on this very street, slaves would unload wares from visiting ships and bring the goods up the hill to this building." She had started speaking again as if the boy were interested in what she had to say.

"And there's the old steamboat dock, Billy, see? Over there by the hotel where we are going to have lunch. Isn't that exciting? You could get on a steamboat at one time in Urbanna and go right up to Baltimore. Imagine that, Billy! History surrounds us in this tiny town. Are you interested in history, son?"

The bone lodged deeper into the lowest cavern of his throat. He thought he might choke as they pulled into the old hotel parking lot, which overlooked the wild marsh splendor and fishing and oyster boats moored on Urbanna Creek. Elizabeth turned off the engine and sat perfectly still. Moments of excruciatingly embarrassing silence passed. Finally, it struck him that she expected him to get out and go around to her side of the car to open the door for her. Without a word, he got out of the car, walked slowly around to her door and performed the gentlemanly act. Sure enough, she delivered a chortle of pleasure. He felt like a dog that had just been taught a new trick, and that she might actually pat him on the head and tell him, "Good dog."

"Thank you, Billy," she said sweetly, taking his hand and giving it a playful squeeze. She was a woman who liked to be pleased. When she was pleased, she was very, very sweet. All the more reason to hate her, he thought.

"How very nice!" she said as the waitress seated them at a table that overlooked the waterfront and handed them menus. "Bring me a glass of soda on ice, please, and a Coke for the young man," she ordered.

"Well, we have something special to celebrate," she said as she pulled a small silver flask from her purse and poured a measure of golden liquid into her soda. She held up her glass to toast him as he sipped his Coke. The rich fragrance of bourbon filled the air suddenly, and Billy breathed it in as if it were an aroma from heaven. He watched as she lifted the bubbly fluid to her lips and took a long drink. He knew only too well the sensation of instant comfort as the whiskey made its way down the throat, the magical numbing of all pain, real or imagined.

Relaxing in her chair, she looked over at him and said again, "You do know about our impending marriage next month, Billy?" He saw her pale blue eyes, magnified in her bifocal glasses, widen with excitement. He thought he could see through her eyes right into the inner chambers of her brain. She looked ugly and old, at least seventy, and he wondered how in the world his father could have fallen for such a woman.

Elizabeth made a supreme effort to keep the conversation going. Billy could see that she was now inspecting him with great interest. She was curious.

"How nice," she said at last, as she sipped her drink. How he wished he could reach out and take the glass from her and finish it off it one large gulp.

Elizabeth smiled sweetly. "Tell, me, Billy, what do you want to do with your life?"

"I don't know. I might be a writer," he said, and saw how her red lipstick had left a thick print on the rim of her glass. It sickened him.

"Oh, don't be foolish," she said with that peculiar chuckle, as if she were laying an egg, as if she had never heard such an outlandish suggestion in all of her seventy-some years. "I mean, what will you do with your life to earn money? That business about writing! Such a life would be just a fancy!"

He said nothing. He was suddenly fascinated with her glass. It seemed she rotated the glass with each sip, so that her lips always touched a fresh part of the glass, like when one takes communion. The grotesque smudges of her lipstick now completely circled the rim, like blood from a fresh wound. Maybe she was feeding her fledglings, Billy thought, fighting a smile, remembering the coat of arms of which she was so proud.

"Your father makes a good living as an engineer, which is a respectable profession, if doctoring does not suit you. God knows not everyone in this world is fit to become a doctor. You could study engineering in college as he did and then come home to Newport News to live and work at the shipyard. Everyone likes it there. Why, half the city works at the shipyard and you could easily get a job there. It's quite the custom that generations of certain families continue to work there year after year. You could be happy and you would make a good living to support a family one day.

"Which means you must do well at Christchurch School in order to qualify for engineering school," she continued. "This means we expect you to work hard and study well and make something of yourself while at Christchurch School."

Their meals had been served, and although Elizabeth had begun to eat, Billy had not touched his food. "You better have something to eat," she said with a stern look of disapproval, pointing to his plate. "And mind your manners. You're soon to be my stepson and I want you to have perfect table manners."

Suddenly ravenously hungry, Billy picked up his fork and dug into the Chesapeake crab cakes and french fries, food that he ordinarily loved to eat. As he gulped down the food, he wondered if his table manners were perfect.

They were not. "Elbows off the table!" she snapped. "And look at the position of your fork! Hold it like this." She demonstrated the proper way a folk should be held, as if he didn't know. "And slow down! You're eating like an animal!"

Elizabeth opened her purse, pulled out her silver flask, and replenished her drink as Billy stared at her with sudden fury. How dare she tell him how to eat? He saw that she was angry too. He stared in fascination as the white skin at her neck turned a bright mottled red. It seemed the obvious truth had finally occurred to her: that she, this strong woman who had always had her way in life, didn't have a chance in hell of ever winning over this boy who would soon become her stepson.

"Let's get this straight once and for all, Billy. If you're to be my stepson, you will learn to uphold certain standards!" she snapped. "If you want to devour your food like a beast when you are not in my presence, that's fine with me. But you will be a gentleman with proper manners when you are with me! Do I make myself clear?"

Elizabeth's face was now contorted in rage. Billy wondered if she would get up from the table and storm out the door, leaving him to get back to Christchurch on his own. But he knew she would not dare to leave him. Not now. That would risk her marriage to his father. Oh, yes, she knew better than to leave him. She had to wait until she safely carried his father's last name before she tried anything as extreme as that.

"Do you like bourbon?" she asked, suddenly relaxing in her chair, almost playfully, apparently having decided to try once again with Billy.

"I prefer vodka, actually," he answered honestly.

She chuckled. "You're going to be quite a handful, aren't you, Billy? Oh, don't think my friends haven't warned me! I'm in my forties, perhaps a bit late for a marriage and family. My life has been solely dedicated to the family, caring for Father, helping my brother run the hospital, keeping his three rambunctious boys in line with a watchful eye and constant advice, taking charge of the nursing school at Mother's death, and of course, keeping my eye on poor Helen and that dreadful man she brought into the family, Rufus."

He said nothing. He had met Rufus and was inclined to agree with her assessment.

"I come from a family with high standards, Billy, and you must meet them, at least while we are together as mother and son. Please," she was suddenly pleading, "could you open your heart and accept this?"

They sat, each looking at each other like two opposing generals before the field of battle. One looked terribly young, innocent, foolish, and vulnerable, rather like a teenager caught with his penis in his hand, and the other wise, clever, undefeatable, and used to withstanding great hardship and irritation as she marched through the many obstacles of life.

"Would you like to drive my car back to school?" she said quite suddenly, in a sugary tone.

"Sure I would!" He jumped up from his chair in anticipation.

She held out the keys to her convertible and jingled them in front of his eyes. "Go ahead, take them. Don't worry, I'll show you how to shift the gears."

It was a bumpy ride up the hill to town with the teenager shifting on brand new gears. At the top of the hill, Billy came to a jolting stop, and then drove around town. By the time he had made several passes up and down Virginia Street, he had finally gotten the hang of the gearshift.

"Not bad," she crooned. "You're a real man now, Billy; you can shift gears and drive a big car!"

"Can I take it across the bridge and drive back to school?"

"Why, sure you can, Billy," she answered, her voice full of honey, and he began to forget the pale, steely, blue eyes with which she watched his every move, the mousy hair with each curl set into her scalp like steel corkscrews, the blue, spidery veins that protruded across the skin on the top of her hands. Maybe she wasn't so bad after all.

On State Route 33 heading back to Christchurch School, he pressed his foot to the accelerator. The car roared down the highway. Elizabeth let out a stifled scream, as if taken by surprise and unable to contain herself. When he pulled into the drive at school, her face was clenched in fright. She looked silly, he thought; disheveled, her lipstick blotched, the hat on her head askew. Her scarf had blown off and snagged on the rearview mirror.

She recovered quickly. A woman who directed a nursing school and helped run a hospital for twenty years could take a little speed every now and then. She chuckled as she rearranged her hat and untangled her scarf. "You're bad, Billy," she said batting her eyelashes as if talking to an old beau. "Just you wait 'til I tell your father how you raced my father's car!"

She reached over and took the keys from the ignition. "I'm glad we've had this little talk, Billy. I think we understand each other now, don't we?" Again she chuckled. He thought how very much she suddenly resembled a great bird just before it ate its freshly caught prey.

Poobah was waiting for Sty when he departed the car, and the two boys walked to the last class together.

"Who was that?"

"Nobody."

"Come on! Everyone says she's going to be your new stepmother! Get any booze during your lunch?"

"Sure, vodka. She drinks it all the time. Straight from the bottle. I really had to work hard to keep up with the old bag."

"Gee, vodka, huh? Serpent's got some beer in his trunk. We'll sneak over to the roadside tavern tonight with the boys and have some fun. Got any cigs?"

"Sure I do. Who wouldn't have cigarettes?"

"All right!"

The two boys slipped into the English classroom on the second floor of Bishop Brown just as the bell rang. Sty sat down in his chair next to the window that faced back to the chapel. He noticed how the afternoon sun filtered down through the leaves, leaving a pattern like bear tracks across the lawn. By God! What beauty! His heart sang with joy at the newfound splendor.

The instructor opened the text to W. B. Yeats and his poem "The Second Coming." Sty listened intently to the words as the instructor recited the poem in the perfect, clipped diction that he had come to expect from prep school faculty. "The falcon cannot hear the falconer . . . " He felt goose bumps tear up and down his arms as his young brain reared up into the fierce words of the poet. Such passion! In a flash, Sty suddenly knew that he could not live his life without such passion. He had to have it. It seemed that the great poet had written those words just for him: Billy Styron. From Newport News, Virginia. Cow town. Now known as Sty, man of the world. Sty cocked his head at some inner voice that was speaking to him. He trembled. Billy Styron! YOU ARE A WRITER!

⌣

Bill, as an adult, had often remembered that classroom from long ago, and that first twinge of awareness of his need to pursue a literary life. Somehow, he had not been surprised. He had already known it, as if the script for his future had already been written for him at birth and it was only a matter of time before he fully understood his literary destiny. It had just taken reading Yeats to nudge him into realizing the glorious truth: "Things fall apart! The center cannot hold!" But, by God, he was not like his mother or father or relatives or friends, or anybody else in the whole of Newport News. He was a writer! A writer! From that day on, young Sty walked toward his secretly known destiny with a determined heart and soul.

CHAPTER 6

Conversations

Bill awoke with a start. A sensation of fear overwhelmed him, and his mind raced as he put initial thoughts into the proper compartments, as a cashier might separate coins in his cash register. Ah, she was dead; it was Saturday evening; the funeral was over, and he had gone to his father's bedroom once again to escape the crowds of well-wishers that still, even now, thronged throughout the house. He had fallen off into a deep, much-needed sleep. He had had too much to drink, he knew that, but how else was he to have survived such a nightmarish day?

He smiled, suddenly remembering the conversation he'd had with Mary. "Write, Mary, write!" he had told her upon first hearing that she thought she might be a writer, too. "How do you know if you are a writer?" she'd asked. Such innocence. He had laughed out loud at her question. What a fine joke . . . How do you know you are a writer!

"You can't be happy without writing," he had answered simply, and they had both laughed at the absurdity of it all, as if anyone could really be happy, pen in hand or not. Yet, writers were foolish enough to think that by holding a pen in hand and pushing heartfelt words across paper, they would at least be delivered a fighting chance.

It had been many years since the question Mary posed had tormented his own mind. He recalled his own voyage of self-discovery—that long, hard journey that one must take to finally understand the special gift and purpose one has to bear in life if one truly is a writer. Bill had told her you had to realize it yourself first, and then you had to hoist your flag wherever you were, announcing to the entire world the startling news that Yes! I'm different; I must write our human story. I don't know why I must do this, but I won't be happy until I do record every living thing that I see and hear and feel that takes place during our times! And then one day, at last, you stop the raving, take up pen and go to war.

"But what would I write about?"

He had laughed uproariously at that point. Such a question! As if he were a teacher and assigning her some homework—"Write about what you did last summer." But then, as she turned her earnest eyes to his, he abruptly stopped laughing. She was serious and he could not hurt this young woman so fresh from Ohio with mere flippancy. After all, she was just beginning her journey. But what should she write about! It seemed like such a ludicrous question— surrounded as she was with such rich characters. "Why, write about your life and your family, Mary. You could never be in want of more interesting material than these very subjects!"

"But won't they be furious with me? I mean, if I write about them, the people that I hold most dear in my heart? Won't they hate me for it?" She looked genuinely alarmed.

"Of course." He drained his remaining ice-laced bourbon and returned briefly to the kitchen bar to refill his drink without missing a beat. "Of course, they will hate you, Mary! Worse than that! Virginians are most terrified of anything they think or do or believe ever going public. If you shine any light on them, if you examine them openly as writers always do, why, they will be furious that you dared betray them in such a vile way!" Replenishing his drink and feeling good for the first time since he had arrived in Newport News, Bill suddenly realized he was enjoying their conversation. He had new hopes that the weekend would not be entirely grim. Perhaps Mary's refreshing supplies of naïveté and enthusiasm could bolster his drooping psyche.

"You should have seen the letters I received after *Lie Down in Darkness*. Why, I could have papered my study with all the hateful mail from well- meaning friends and family! They told me what they thought of me and my first book for my own good, of course." Bill smiled as Mary took in all that he had to say like a new believer standing at the altar of God.

"I don't think I would want to hurt anybody with my writing," she said.

He laughed again. "Novelists write the truth the way they see it. That's our gift. That's our job. It's our only job! You and I have the right to write about the world the way we see it. The world has to accept our right. They don't have to read our books, but they have to tolerate our right to tell our stories the way we see fit. And if we are not willing to take on this responsibility and hard work—and believe me, Mary, writing is really hard work—then we have no business taking up our pen!"

"I suppose I could fictionalize everything," she offered.

He had stared hard at her. "There is no fiction, Mary. Everything a writer writes, he has seen and felt and heard in this great big world. Remember that."

The fragments of conversation with Mary, remembered with such enjoyment, as if each word had been a choice piece of candy to be relished, ended as Veala called his name. He looked up at her with a startled expression. "Would you like something to eat, Mr. Bill? You have been laughing in your sleep."

He groaned, suddenly remembering his dream, and then his conversation with Mary, both intertwined into such complicated patterns. He felt weak, lifeless, and confused from all his hard-pressed emotions. It was all too much. One moment he was a desperately vulnerable fifteen-year-old boy whose entire life was unraveling, and then the next, juxtaposed on top of such misery, a successful forty-four-year-old author back in his father's bed, his hated stepmother dead.

"You need some food, Mr. Bill. I've brought you a mug of black coffee and a ham sandwich. It's your favorite, Smithfield brand. Remember—what I used to make for you when you were a boy coming home from prep school for vacations? Here, let me plump a few pillows for you so you can sit up and see the view of the water as you eat. Just like when you were a boy."

As Veala gathered extra pillows and adjusted them against his back, he managed to break away from his web of anguished memories and sit up in bed. He looked around the room and Elizabeth's oppressive presence returned. Her funeral had been this weekend. She was dead and buried, her face turned up in the coffin, her hands folded in prayer across her breast, and she was out of his life forever. He was free at last, but why was it that he still felt in her steely grip?

"A gentleman by the name of Mr. Tom Master came by. He asked about you. Said he was an old friend from Christchurch School."

"Tom Master! Better known at school as Ol' Beak! Is he still here?"

"No, he said to call tomorrow—if you have time to meet up with him, that is. I told him you were leaving on Sunday."

"Tom came with me to the wedding!"

Veala looked confused. "Why, what wedding are you talking about, Mr. Bill?"

He stared at her, as if trying to understand her question. "What wedding? Why, my father and Elizabeth's wedding; you remember, you were there, too. Who else's wedding would I be remembering?"

"Oh, well, that was almost thirty years ago, Mr. Bill! That's all behind you now. Better to just forget all about it."

"Forget it? How can I forget it? That woman! She almost destroyed me."

"Now, now, Mr. Bill, that poor woman is dead. You know she did the best she could. No sense in remembering bad things about the deceased, is there now?"

"It's amazing I was ever able to write, Veala. Why, if that woman had gotten her hold on me even a few years earlier, she would have completely done me in. Made a doctor out of me! A lawyer! An engineer! For God's sake! Selected my wife! Set me up in a house in the proper neighborhood! Christened my children at St. Paul's Church! Had me playing golf at the James River Country Club! Gotten me into the German and the Hampton Yacht Club! My God! There's no end to what she might have done!" He shuddered, realizing how narrowly he had escaped such a life.

"Well, you have certainly managed to write now, Mr. Bill. No one can argue that. I read all your books, too! I'm proud that I know you and that I helped raise you. Be grateful you were able to set out on a life of your own, Mr. Bill. Think of all of us who love you and are caught in the town we were born in, never able to get away. It's best to let the past go, Mr. Bill."

"What writer ever lets go of the past? It's food for future novels!"

Veala sighed. "Nothing has changed, Mr. Bill. I never could talk any sense into you, that's for sure! And neither could Mrs. Styron either, for that matter." She chuckled.

"I've been having the worst nightmares."

"Why don't you come downstairs? There's still some family there. That Mr. Chip and his young wife from Ohio, is it Miss Mary? The one you were chatting with before and after the funeral? Oh, Mr. Bill, it was such fun watching Miss Rose and her trying on Mrs. Styron's hats! It's been a long time since we heard that kind of laughter in this house, that's for sure!"

"I quite agree, Veala."

"The ladies absolutely refused the white gloves I offered them, Mr. Bill. 'After all, it is 1969,' they said. 'Women need not appear everywhere in white gloves, as if their hands were too refined to ever risk touching anything earthly.' I laughed and laughed, Mr. Bill! But if Mrs. Styron had heard such conversations going on in her very own bedroom, she would have turned over in her grave!"

"There were plenty of white gloves at the funeral; 1969 or not, this is the South. They don't budge when it comes to tradition. I saw them all waving at me, those draped hands, like flags of surrender, those hundreds of fidgeting, feminine hands from generations of excellent Virginia breeding, all their hands properly sheathed in white cloth and waving at me when I passed by the pews."

"What a lot of nonsense, Mr. Bill! You haven't changed one bit. Now, here, have some coffee. It'll make you feel a lot better. I understand you'll be leaving in the morning, then? That you have a speaking engagement in New York Monday evening?"

"Right, Veala. You know, it was only after the wedding that she totally changed and war between us was officially declared."

"What war? Whatever are you talking about, Mr. Bill?"

Bill took a long gulp of Veala's good black coffee and lay back on his pillow. He guessed there was no sense in trying to explain things to Veala. But evil his stepmother was, and wily too, he thought; evil in her desire to take over a vulnerable fifteen-year-old boy and mold him into a figure of her pleasing, and wily to cleverly hide her behavior so that he was the only person to see it. Oh yes, she had been far craftier than his dream had allowed.

As if she had heard his thoughts, Veala reached down and patted his arm tenderly, in a motherly way. After all that had happened over the years, Veala had been the only one to provide Billy with any inkling of maternal love in those years following the wedding.

"You must have had a really bad dream, Mr. Bill. You look as if you've seen a ghost. But enough of all that. I'm going back downstairs now to check on your father. He's tired, Mr. Bill. You can't leave him to face all the guests by himself. Why, all those nuns from the hospital are here. And dozens of the old Buxton nurses that Mrs. Styron once taught at the hospital have come over. One woman—she must have been a hundred years old—recalled the old hospital and Mrs. Styron's father, Dr. Joseph. He ran the place like a ship, Mr. Bill. Took care of our people too, he did, and never charged a dime. He was a mighty fine man. Then that old nurse, she stood before me and drew herself up proudly and said: 'I knew the first Dr. Buxton and I was the nurse chosen to stay with him at the hospital the last weeks of his life. Every morning he would awaken at six, and he would say, 'Where's my son, Russell? Is he at the hospital yet?' And, of course, he hadn't arrived yet and we all had to assure the old doctor that his son was at the hospital and busy taking care of all the patients. And then, finally, around nine A.M., Dr. Russell would come up to see his father, and his father would go over the duties for the day.' Imagine that, Mr. Bill. Dr. Russell living in such a stern environment as all that!"

"Oh, I can imagine it, all right, Veala. And I did much more than just imagine it, too. As you well know, I lived the same kind of life, because you were here; you saw it, too. Elizabeth spent years trying to make a doctor out of me. You know, even though she graduated from Hollins, in those days not many women went off to medical school. She wanted to become a doctor just like her brother, but her father would not have it. 'Become a nurse as is proper for your gender, and help your mother run the nursing school,' is what Dr. Joseph told her."

Veala's interest waned; Bill could see in her face that she was tired. Really tired, perhaps beyond the white man's ability to understand. It had been an even longer day for her, taking care of the family, as she did every day of her life. He knew that she had a life of her own, that her family was waiting for her to come home at last from his white world, to feed and care for them. And why should she really care about doctors and hospitals and all the family squabbles involved with such enterprises, and how impossible it was for a fifteen-year-old boy to live with such people? Veala had her own world with its many problems to solve. How could she possibly take on any more?

"I'm off now, Mr. Bill. Is there anything else you need before I go?" He waved her off and she picked up the empty plate and cup and left. He hoped she could merely deposit the dishes in the kitchen, say good night to the family, and depart out the back door for her home at last.

Bill's spirits immediately returned to his previous depressed state, what he always called "the black dog," after a pub he had once visited. Later, he had read that Winston Churchill had always referred to his depression as "the black dog." The term had always struck him as the perfect sobriquet for his own struggle with depression, and he had begun using it even in his writings and speech.

He realized he wanted a drink. He arose from the bed, changed into fresh clothes, crept down the back stairs, poured a swift slosh of bourbon over a few chunks of ice, and slipped out to the screened back porch. Ah, nobody had heard him. He would have more time for solace. He settled in a deck chair to enjoy his drink.

The back garden was draped in dusk, the magnolia in full bloom dominating all the other trees, like a queen at her court of maples, pecans, plums, dogwoods, and crepe myrtles, with a sprinkling of white pine along the border. Along the foundation of the house spread the typical Tidewater shrubbery: azalea, camellia, and creamy white gardenias, now in bloom and filling the night air with heady perfume. The scent was heavy, and as it mixed with the fumes of Uncle Jack right under his nose, he twitched with pleasure.

Great clouds in the shapes of dragons, prehistoric birds, and poodles united to sweep across the already launched full moon. He focused his senses to hear the night noise punctuated with sounds of human conversation and laughter from the parlor. Cicadas and tree frogs sang in the night, as though celebrating some grand piece of news, and a cardinal called to her young. A pair of doves cooing intermittently in the night, along with the soft hoot of an owl perched high in a tree, lent the last notes to the symphony.

Bill heard more sounds as his senses expanded to more distant realms. There were sounds from Hampton Roads, too, and although from the back porch there was no direct view of the water, he could still hear an occasional fishing boat distantly buzzing along the shore, or a lonely gull calling out his last mournful cry in the dark night.

Closer were the sounds of the city. Chesapeake Avenue, a busy highway that ran past the front of the house and separated it from the shore, had traffic at all hours. Although the rush hour had long waned, he could still hear the periodic swoosh of an occasional car and see the sweep of its headlight as they flashed across the backyard.

More horrifying thoughts pricked his brain. He was that tender boy once again, lying under blankets of despair in the back upstairs bedroom, helplessly watching the headlights of yesterday as they swept across the ceiling in his bedroom. With little preparation for what Jane Austen had warned was the "stuff of life"—those many hardships that lay ahead for children; second marriages and all they entailed for the young, innocent victims—he now realized he had been engaged in a fight for the survival of his very own soul.

CHAPTER 7

The Wedding

During that first month at Christchurch School, Tom Master, a local boy who lived in Urbanna and attended the school as a day student, became Sty's best friend. Because of the close proximity of Tom's home to the school, Sty would often go home with him on weekends. This helped relieve a dull ache that stemmed from a desperate sense of loneliness, an agonizing awareness of wanting to go home that had settled into his chest like a case of influenza, making every breath of air a difficult task.

Yet school was going well enough, and Sty was not only enjoying his classes, but learning how to play tennis. He soon discovered that, with his light frame and lightning serve, he could become an ace in at least one sport.

The only dark cloud in the sky was the upcoming wedding. The thought of it hung off the horizon like an approaching storm, ready to strike at any moment and ruin the day. Sty sometimes spoke to Tom of this coming horror and, at the last minute, invited Tom to accompany him.

"It'll be for laughs," Sty told him as they met the headmaster, who was scheduled to drive them to the wedding at St. Paul's Church in downtown Newport News, about a seventy-mile journey south. They were dressed in their school's navy sports coats with the school emblem sewn into the front pocket, set off by white shirts and the school's striped navy blue and orange tie.

"At least we get away from school for a day," Tom whispered to Sty as they climbed into the car. Tom noticed his friend was unusually quiet. Sty looked like he was on his way to the dentist to have a tooth pulled, rather than traveling to a gala event.

"The important thing is for you boys to remember to mind your manners," Headmaster Smith said as he settled himself behind the wheel. "Remember, you represent Christchurch School when you are out in public."

He reached over to straighten Sty's tie, stared him hard in the eye with an expression well-honed from his military background, as if daring him to pull any crass stunts at his father's wedding, and whisked an imaginary piece of lint from Sty's new navy blazer.

He leaned back and nodded approvingly, taking both boys into his gaze. "You look good, my boys. I'm proud of you." They settled into back seats and proceeded south to Newport News. It was a quiet trip spent mostly gazing out at the passing fields of corn. When they crossed the city line, fragments of suburb and city popped up like mushrooms along the side of the road. The boys had nothing to say.

The car pulled up in front of St. Paul's at two P.M., exactly an hour before the service was to begin. "The reception is at the James River Country Club. I'll be right at the front entrance of the club at six P.M. sharp to take you back to school. Be there. Don't make me have to come looking for you," he added and drove off.

Sty looked at his watch. They had an hour to kill before the service would start. "What should we do now, Tom?"

"Easy." Tom pulled out some vodka in a silver flask he replenished from his father's supplies every time he went home on weekends. He offered Sty a swig, and his friend took a good, long swallow.

"The good thing about vodka is no one can smell it on your breath," Tom said with a knowing look, as if he were an expert on such matters. Sty took another long swallow and then grinned broadly as the fiery substance made its way down his throat.

"How much you got?"

"Plenty. This flask and another in my back pocket."

"Are you sure they won't smell it on our breath?"

"Hell, no. Why do you think everyone in the South drinks vodka?"

He took another deep swig and passed the flask back to Tom. "Pretty good stuff!"

"Let's have a cigarette," Tom said, opening a fresh pack of Lucky Strikes. "The best part of a cigarette is lighting up in the breeze. You got to do it like this." Tom turned his back to the wind, cupped his hands, struck the match and inhaled deeply. "Just like Bogie does it in the movies," he said with a grin.

The boys tried the church door but found it was still locked, so they sat down on the front steps to wait for some action, smoking their cigarettes and trading swigs of vodka. The first sign of life appeared in the form of a sexton, dressed in a black flowing robe and hurrying down the street toward them. He saw the boys and looked worried. "You boys here for the wedding?" he asked, looking directly at the cigarettes.

"Sure. I'm Mr. Styron's son here from prep school," Sty said, remembering to rise. "This is my friend from school, Tom Master."

"Good. Look, if I were you, I'd get rid of those cigarettes. Your father just pulled up in the parking lot behind the church. It doesn't look good to see young boys smoking on the front steps of church."

They sank their half-smoked stubs in the dirt and followed the sexton inside the massive stone church. It was cool, with numerous dark recesses where the sunlight that streamed in from the large stained glass window at the front of the church failed to reach. Sty sought the darkness and knew that was where he wanted to sit.

Already people were arriving at the church, and the seats were filling up fast. He saw his neighbor, old Mrs. Westcott, whom he had scared last summer with a black snake he'd caught in the garden.

His father approached, dressed in a tuxedo. "I want to talk to you, son," he said, motioning Billy to follow. He led him back to a room behind the altar. Choir robes hung lifelessly, suspended on wires, like white angels in heaven.

"I loved your mother, Billy," he said, looking slightly embarrassed. Billy blinked a sudden tear forcibly back into his eye. "But Elizabeth, she is quite a socially prominent woman, son. It's an opportunity for me. I'll be part of a big, important family and have companionship and never be lonely again."

Billy said nothing but suddenly saw in his father's face that he had a profound need to be better than he thought he was.

"My love for Elizabeth in no way changes my love for your mother or for you, Billy. I want you to know that."

A sudden sob came forth from the old man's tightened lips, and he flung his arms around his son and hugged him so long that Billy squirmed. "There," he said, finally releasing him from his tight embrace "Just remember, this marriage will have many advantages for you, too."

Billy turned away from his father.

"One more thing, son. I will always love you."

An organist had begun playing the muted chords of a prelude. Billy turned and walked back to the sanctuary, which had now filled almost to capacity. Tom was seated in a back pew with a smirk on his face.

"Did you get the 'I love you' shit?" he whispered.

"Sure."

"Well, he does, I guess. In his way. It must be something parents have to say to their kids while stabbing them in the back. I know that's what happened in my case, anyway."

"Stupid," Billy muttered. The boys settled into the back pew, in the darkest corner they could find.

The stragglers were now hurrying to find the last vacant seats. Soon every seat was taken and every neck craned to see or be seen, as happens in Southern society. Elizabeth had told Billy earlier it would be the wedding of the year. He looked around and thought he had never seen so many ridiculous hats. It was as if he were on an island surrounded by a sea of bobbing flowerpots.

"You're to be seated in the front pew with family, Billy," an usher appeared to deliver whispered orders.

"I'm fine here."

"I'm afraid Miss Buxton won't allow you to sit here. You're soon to be her stepson. You must be seated in the front pew as family."

"I won't move," Billy hissed at the man. The usher's face had turned a deep shade of red. Why does she care where I sit? Billy wondered, but then felt a pounding sensation, like someone was punching him in his chest. He looked up and saw every eye in the church on him. The usher shot a look of concern to the back of the church and shifted his weight from one black shiny shoe to the other.

Another usher arrived at his pew, and then another. "She won't start the processional until Billy moves to the front pew," the second usher whispered urgently.

That was when Billy saw her peeking out from the door at the back of the church. He sat for some time, refusing to move. He could feel her eyes on the back of his neck and his skin began to burn where she was staring. He had visions of three ushers carrying him kicking and screaming to the front pew, and then tying him down. He guessed they could find some rope that they kept on hand for such occasions at the last minute, if they had to. It would certainly offer the congregation a show they would never forget, and by all means become the wedding of the year.

Father came out with the rector from a door at the right of the altar and stood attentively at the front of the aisle. The organist ended her prelude. Soon even Father and the rector had joined the others in turning their eyes on him.

Billy realized he was committing the worst possible sin in Virginia society: mortifying Elizabeth in public. The thought elated him, and it seemed that hours passed as he relished in its glow. Suddenly Tom poked him in the ribs. "Move, Sty," he said, his voice so loud and husky that it resonated through the church.

Shocked at his friend's treachery, Billy stood up out of the darkness. An usher grabbed his arm and propelled him along to the front pew, fully lit in all its glory. He sat down with a terrible thunk, as if someone had just dropped a frozen carcass in the pew designated for family.

A sigh of relief seemed to move through the church as the moment of dreadful awkwardness passed. All eyes moved to the rector. The organist began Mendelssohn's glorious wedding march. Elizabeth walked down the aisle on the arm of her brother, Dr. Russell, and Billy saw that brother and sister looked just alike. There was the sound of weeping in the church. The crazy sister, Helen, was sitting behind him, crying into her handkerchief. She was always crying about something, maybe joined by some of the old nurses her mother had once taught, or maybe some of the old patients Dr. Joseph had cared for, now teetering on their last legs. Who knew what such nutty people felt? Billy thought.

He didn't hear a word of the ceremony. But as his eyes fell on Elizabeth's radiant face, he saw how happy she looked. She glowed. Nobody could have missed that. Disgusting. He thought his father looked silly, too, like he'd just been swallowed and was surprised to suddenly find himself in a stomach. Billy finally gave up looking and concentrated on a candle in the candelabra on the left side of the altar. It was the safest place for him to look.

Finally, the ceremony ended, and Billy was swept out of the church amidst the joyous throng and into a waiting car to head for the reception at the James River Country Club. There, in the ornate foyer, he was able to make contact with Tom again. They moved away from the exuberant crowds to the golf museum in an anteroom off the lobby, where pictures of dozens of Scottish golf clubs were on display, along with historical golf equipment. The boys cast disinterested looks at the things that adults hold so dear before lighting up cigarettes and polishing off the last of the vodka.

"Where are they going on their honeymoon?" Tom asked, with a teasing expression.

"Who cares?"

"How long are they going to be gone?"

"How should I know?"

"Do you think they'll do it? Do you? If you ask me, they look far too old for that sort of business."

"I doubt it. Who would think of sex around that old witch? He's probably just marrying her as a favor, so she can finally say she landed a husband before she dropped dead."

"Come on, let's get some food. I'll bet it's a big spread." Tom led the way through the double doors to the back of the country club, which overlooked the James River. A long table covered with sumptuous food stretched across the entire side of the room.

"You're a mighty lucky young man to have landed in her family," about a thousand people said to Billy as he and Tom made their way through the crowds of hideous people with beaked noses, bulging eyes, and flushed faces, all dressed in their finery. The boys reached the food and ravenously began stuffing it down as fast as they could.

Billy felt her claws dig into his shoulders in front of the fried chicken. There was no mistaking that evil touch, and he knew who it was before even turning his head. "Turn for a picture with me and smile, Billy," she said, positioning them both in front of a cameraman. Flashes popped.

"You didn't smile, Billy! Take the picture again! We will wait for a smile from my young man." The photographer waited while she beamed into the camera. Billy wondered if he looked pleasant. Somehow he doubted it. He was sure he looked about as pleasant as a storm racing down the James River on a summer's day. The photographer took a few more shots and then sauntered off into the crowd.

"You've been smoking at my wedding, you hateful little beast," she whispered in his ear.

He stared at her. He saw her as she was, an evil woman, a wicked witch, a sorceress from the deepest and vilest quarters of the world who had devoured his weak father and was now hungry for young flesh.

"I saw how you tried to ruin my wedding!" she hissed in his ear. "You will pay dearly for your behavior!" And then, pasting a sudden radiant smile on her face, she whirled to face her pressing society.

He heard music; a string quartet in the corner had started up what sounded like "The Blue Danube." Oh, no! Mother had loved "The Blue Danube!" It was her favorite piece! She had a collection of the Strauss waltzes and played them often on the old Victrola in the dining room. He remembered how she and Father would jump up from their chairs when "The Blue Danube" came on and waltz around the room. He felt sickened that Elizabeth had ordered his mother's favorite piece to be played at her wedding.

He saw how the traitor came to his new wife now and asked her to dance with him. Oh, vile man! So short of memory, so long in deceit! He saw the champagne glasses passed around and heard the laughter and good cheer. He managed to purloin a glass off a round silver tray as the server passed it. They were ordered to raise glasses with clenched fists, in a gaggle of happy toasts and smiling faces. A cake was sliced and there was some foolishness about Elizabeth and Father sharing a piece. Nauseating! Then the waitstaff delivered pieces all around. Who felt like eating wedding cake? Stupid! What Billy wanted was another glass of champagne. He managed to get three more refills before Elizabeth caught sight of him sucking them down on the sidelines faster than a hog eats corn. She shot right over to the server and, pointing at Billy, hissed a few cross words. Billy had a feeling he was not going to get any more of the bubbly water. No matter. He was already feeling pretty good. The few glasses he had swallowed got him through the reception. What more could a young man have asked for on such a bleak day?

After what seemed like hours, it was time to leave. By God, the woman threw her bouquet of flowers to the adoring crowd as if she were some young nymph. And there was such laughter! What in the world was so funny? Was there something wrong with these people that they had to laugh like hyenas at a wedding? No man had ever had to suffer as much as he did!

Tom came to his side. "Let's go, Sty. It's time to meet Headmaster Smith."

They slipped out the side door and over to the front entrance. The headmaster had already arrived, and as soon as he spotted the boys, he pulled his car to the front door. Thank God he was right on the dot, Sty thought, getting into the back seat of the car. No one was ever late at Christchurch.

Lateness was for those who would be flops in life. Being on time was a religion. One had to be first on time; then one could become a success and then die and go to heaven.

Sty slept most of the way on the trip back to Christchurch. The headmaster tried hard to spark some conversation with the couple of brooding teenagers stretched out in the backseat. No go. Neither Tom nor Sty felt like talking. Whether he realized his two charges were drunk, neither really knew. At least he was far enough away from the boys that he could not smell the champagne on their breath. By the time they reached school, the pair had slept off most of the damage.

Sty may have been asleep, but he had turned one sentence over and over in his mind: I don't have to see her again until Thanksgiving. He thanked God, in whom he so ardently disbelieved, for the greatest blessing of the year.

CHAPTER 8

Thanksgiving

Even safely ensconced in prep school, far away from that woman, Sty did not know how he would survive the year. He would awaken in the night remembering that his mother was dead and that a stepmother had wormed her way into his life. Gasping for breath in the darkness, he felt as though he were drowning at sea. The pain in his chest settled deep in his heart, causing a constant ache. He was busy with school activities, but when the lights went out and the dorm quieted as the bell tower tolled its last chimes of the day, the hurt was unbearable.

He thought that his stepmother wanted to steal him from his rightful mother and remake him into her sweet little Billy. Worse, she wanted to turn him into a Buxton, which could never be done. He sensed it, just as a dog, upon seeing the veterinarian's stealthy approach, knows it is about to be put down and casts soulful eyes up to its master. He sympathized with the dog, feeling he had been thrown into a similar situation with his father's remarriage. Only his was a life-and-death struggle for his soul.

He lived a good part of his life in dreams. When things became too stressful or difficult, he simply withdrew into the cool, grey realm of his brain. He could slide across that sea at a moment's calling, his sails stretched to their limits in the wind, or sweep, wing on wing, through the starry sky to the ends of the universe.

School was good; he was enjoying his classes and instructors, and he had lined up a few close friends. But when he went home to Newport News for a holiday or weekend, Sty had to stay on alert against his stepmother's constant schemes to remake him into her little Billy. Even though he remained aloof, he noticed everything: the way her pale blue eyes dropped to the zipper of his pants to make sure it was in the up position every time he walked into the room; the way she called colored folk "neegras"; how Veala winced when she called her "my good girl"; the way she inspected her teeth or patted her hair every time she passed the mirror in the foyer; how she batted her eyes at the rector when he came to visit; or how she looked at poor ruddy-faced Rufus, her sister's late-stab-at-life husband, as if he were dirt under her feet.

Sty saw that she manipulated his father, as Southern wives tended to do; and also her brother; his wife; her other siblings; nephews; the rector; neighbors; the garbage collector; various repairmen who came to fix things; Veala's husband, who delivered and then picked up his wife in his old truck at the back door at the end of each day; nurses and staff at the hospital; and every other man, woman, or child who crossed her path. Sty swore she would never manipulate him.

Every detail of her person was recorded in his brain, as if some massive iron stamp had left its imprint on him forever. He imagined that one day he would write of her; yes, he would make her a leading character in a book and show the world what she was really like under all the trimmings of her fancy Tidewater society.

"How are things going at home?" Headmaster Smith asked him one day in November as Sty was changing classes. Sty did not respond. "Well, son," the headmaster said, putting his arm around Sty's shoulder, "I know that sometimes changes in life are not easy to adjust to. My best advice is to talk things over with your father on your next weekend home."

That would be Thanksgiving, and as the weeks wound down to holiday dismissal and the other boys were joyously preparing for their vacation away from school, Sty prepared for the bleak week he expected at home. He had the perfect opportunity to speak to his father as he came alone to pick Sty up from school.

In that two-hour drive home, Billy found himself telling his father how unhappy he was with the woman who had been foisted into his life. He surprised himself with the hot barrage of bitter words that shot forth from his mouth.

"Now son, try to understand. Elizabeth is late in life to have married. I never knew how difficult it might be for a woman in her mid-forties, who had never been married, to suddenly have a husband, much less a teenage son, and all this along with her career. Be kind, son. This experience has not been easy for her."

"I hate her!" Billy said, his voice cracking and his eyes welling up with tears. He immediately regretted his words, for his father gasped, and Billy saw a wall of despair come over him, as it had on the morning his mother had died.

"Try, son, try to love her, if only for my sake."

That was the end of the conversation. Father and son rode on in silence. Billy resolved never again to tell his father his feelings about that woman, but to keep them locked safely in his heart.

There was one bright spot over Thanksgiving break. Billy happened to discover a book on human anatomy in the hospital library, where he would occasionally go to curl up with a volume. The book, from Elizabeth's nursing school days, was filled with detailed diagrams of sexual organs. He soon learned he could quite easily filch it from the library simply by slipping it into his shirt and carrying it home for a good read. Trying to figure out what happened with such mysterious bodily equipment was a constant source of fascination. What delight to gaze on the many illustrations of sexual organs, especially the mysterious vaginas, uteri, fallopian tubes, and clitorises.

No one had ever mentioned anything about sex to Billy at home; he had been left on his own to try to figure the mystery out for himself. Beyond shady talk and the constant stream of innuendos in the dorm at school, where his friends dropped hints that they were fully experienced in the ways of wild women, sex was a complete puzzle. Without Elizabeth's book on human anatomy, it was questionable whether he would have ever had any legitimate sex education.

But staring at diagrams of vaginas all day long while huddled in his bedroom was hardly enough to sate his expanding curiosity. Girls were on his mind day and night. Billy discovered that Thanksgiving week was an excellent time to take long walks on Chesapeake Avenue in search of women. Any kind of woman would do: big, little, young, old, white, black, blonde, redheaded, long nosed, pug nosed, slender ankled, stocky framed, morose, giggling, whatever; he cared not what kind of woman he might meet. All he wanted was a female.

Billy soon realized some women had a certain look in their eyes if they were interested in him in that way. Billy constantly wondered: would she do it with me? He imagined the passion, fury, and glory of it at least a dozen times a day.

That week, Elizabeth walked into his bedroom as usual, without so much as a three-second-warning rap on the door, and discovered him reading her old book on anatomy. It must have triggered hope in her that this was a sign that he was interested in becoming a doctor because a lecture was forthcoming on making something of his life. "Would you be interested in becoming a doctor, Billy?" she asked coyly. "If so, my brother would be happy to take you to the hospital to view a surgery."

Billy had already heard that the family thought this was the best test for determining a young boy's aptitude for medicine. He had heard that Dr. Joseph had once taken his young son, Russell, to the hospital to test whether he would follow in his footsteps, and returned with the good news that a new surgeon was emerging in the family. Billy realized, with a sinking heart, that he was at just the right age to stand the test.

"Never!" he shouted, not caring how crazy he might have sounded. "View a surgery! Blood! Spilled guts! Bright purple and green innards spreading across the sheets!" Billy blanched and almost gagged right there in front of his hovering stepmother. He felt he was a baby turtle just hatched, on a furtive run to the sea, descended upon by a starving gull with a very sharp beak.

"I'm going to be a writer!" Billy said, finally recovering from the terrifying image. With quivering hands balled up into two white fists at his sides, he tried hard to appear nonchalant about his declaration, though he felt they could have been the most important words that he had ever spoken to an adult in his life.

The beak tore into the tender flesh. "Are you still talking about becoming a writer?" She said this, rolling her blue eyes as usual, as if she had just uttered the filthiest word ever known to man. "Be practical, Billy! There is no money in writing. How would you support yourself? What kind of life could a Bohemian ever provide for his family?"

Silence descended on the room like fog, as it did in all conversations between them.

"I understand you've had a few of your stories selected for the school literary magazine," she continued, clearly hoping not to lose Billy to his usual descent into silence. A new look of amusement suddenly flooded her face, like she had never heard anything so entertaining in all her life. The hideous beak savaged the warm morsels of flesh and savored them one by one.

"That's good, son. We're proud of you," his father said, suddenly appearing at the bedroom door. "Writing is a wonderful gift, something you inherited from your mother. She was both artistic and creative. But Elizabeth has a point, son. You must think of the skill to write as a hobby, and not as your life's work."

"Time for refreshments!" Elizabeth trilled gaily, joyful in victory, as if mere food would cure all family disagreements. Billy and his father followed her downstairs, where good ol' Veala appeared with a tray of homemade cookies and a pitcher of lemonade, as she always seemed to do at every difficult time in his life. Elizabeth, a fake smile pasted across her face, soon filled the parlor with trumped-up good cheer as she triumphantly presided over the conversation.

The good cheer did not last long, however. Elizabeth reached into her pocket and drew out Billy's report card, which had just arrived in the mail. "Well, let's see," she said, watching his face flush a deep red. "A good grade in English—if one considers a B good, that is—but the math, science, and history scores will never do, Billy."

Billy sat down on the horsehair Victorian loveseat as both adults flanked him. He felt the sharp filling prick at his legs from beneath its velvet cover. Not comfortable with his position between both adults, he quickly stood up and instead made his way to the pantry.

"Where are you going, young man?" Elizabeth called after him. He ignored her. "You come back here! You're not to leave the room when your father and I are speaking to you!"

He stooped down and opened the cabinet where his father kept his whiskey. In a flash, he had the top off a bottle of vodka and poured a good draught into his glass of lemonade. Veala watched him from her position at the sink and clucked her disapproval like a brooding hen. He flashed a quick smile, put his finger to his lips to warn her that this was strictly a secret between them, and slipped into the washroom off the pantry to flush the toilet.

"Sorry. I had to use the facility," Billy said, rejoining the scowling pair with his well-spiked drink raised in toast.

"You're not to use the pantry bathroom!" Elizabeth snapped. "That bathroom is for Veala! How many times must I tell you we do not use the same facilities as the help?" She rolled her eyes in disgust at such imbecility. "But then, perhaps," she added unkindly, "that would be asking too much of you, considering the shabby way in which you were raised!"

"Now, now, Elizabeth," his father interrupted. "No sense in becoming upset, my dear."

Billy took a generous swig of his hard-laced lemonade, then finished it in one huge gulp. Perhaps he had learned how to cope with the unpleasantness in life from his stepmother? Earlier in the week, hadn't he walked into the kitchen, as Elizabeth was entertaining Dr. Russell and his first wife, Red, over drinks in the living room? He had seen her tear open a new bottle of bourbon, uncap the bottle, hold it to her nose, and deeply inhale the heady aroma. A satisfied sigh had escaped her lips, as if she had suddenly been embraced by a choir of angels. Then she poured the whiskey straight into her glass, no water, no soda, not even a few cubes of ice. She had held it to her lips and chugged it down in several long gulps.

He must have made a slight noise, because she had whirled around and gasped, "Why, you little snoop!" Billy had withdrawn quickly up the back steps to his bedroom, his usual path of retreat, but he had learned a secret. His stepmother enjoyed the taste and smell of whiskey, just as much as he did.

"You are going to have to settle down, young man, and apply yourself at school." Elizabeth broke into his thoughts while shaking his report card at him. But the vodka had emboldened him. He rose from the sofa and, with sudden strength and determination, strode out the front door. He was across Chesapeake Avenue before she could even react. He wanted far horizons: freedom, escape, Hampton Roads, the bay, the sea, the majestic star-studded sky that would comfort him.

Billy stood on the shore, taking in the evening world of calm water as the sun sank in the western sky. The sea was cool and shimmering in pinks and greys, like silk in the glow of candlelight. He kicked off his shoes and felt the sand, still warm under his bare feet from the mild Tidewater day.

His eyes followed the path of a lone gull that flew toward the west into the last light of day. Soon the gull disappeared, only to be replaced by an egret, soaring low along the shore and crying its soulful call.

Billy gazed at the water, yearning suddenly, in some inexplicable way, for its comforting depths. He thought of the boy who had drowned in the Rappahannock River during the early years of Christchurch School. He wondered if perhaps that boy, too, had just been given a stepmother, and the drowning had not been an accident. Maybe he had sought the cool riverbed as a safe region where a boy might give up the trials and tribulations of life and lie down to rest forever.

He saw her on the beach, partially hidden in the skeletal remains of an uprooted tree. She was blonde, slender, and very pale, like an apparition, and his eyes settled on her outstretched hand that rested on her knee. He saw how her fingers were extended, like feathers in the wind. Billy, mesmerized, began to walk toward her, pulled by some invisible force.

In the failing light his eyes could still make out the gentle curve of her neck, the cast of her slight shoulders, and the way she was seated on the log with her legs pulled in neatly under her tucked skirt.

But who was she? Billy had never seen the girl before. As he approached, he saw that her dress was a pale blue with soft fluffy ruffles around her white neck.

He drew closer to her, his eyes now focusing on her bare foot weaving back and forth in the shallow water, holding his breath for fear that she was merely a dream and that she would float away at any moment, like a wisp of cloud in the night sky. But was she real? He didn't think he could bear the loss if the exquisite girl he saw on the log was only a dream.

Billy sat down on the log and reached for her hand. He was trembling. He gently put his arm around her shoulder and impetuously leaned over to kiss her lips.

"I love you," he whispered hoarsely, now folding both of his arms around her, hoping to hold her to him forever, his entire being filled with a sudden glowing and overwhelming sensation.

"Billy!" that woman's voice shrieked from her front porch across the avenue. "I see you over there huddled on the beach! Come home! It's late and time to lock the house!"

He considered ignoring Elizabeth's abrupt summons, but he knew that would only trigger another mortifying round of shouts. Rising miserably from his ecstasy in the sand, he looked again at his beautiful girl to bid her farewell. But she was gone. He turned to study the shoreline in both directions but saw no sign of her. Aching, he started home. He could feel rage burning inside his lungs, heart, and stomach, as though he had swallowed a vial of acid.

"What an inconsiderate young man you are!" Elizabeth fumed as he passed her wordlessly at the front door and trudged up the stairs. "I'll bet your selfish behavior caused the death of your poor, dear mother!" When he did not answer, she became even angrier. "You think of no one but yourself!"

He heard a door open across the hall and his father's voice calling her from the front upstairs bedroom they shared. "Now, now, Elizabeth; no need to be upset. Boys will be boys, you know. Now come to bed, my dear."

Billy gently shut the door to his bedroom. I have lived through Thanksgiving, he thought. Tomorrow he would return to school. Tom's parents would pick him up right after breakfast, and he would be safely back in his dorm by noon. He could forget this hellhole until Christmas vacation.

He stood by the window and saw the first evening stars twinkling in the sky. He gazed at the neighboring house overlooking their backyard and saw the upstairs bedrooms still lit. Could the girl he'd seen on the beach be in one of those rooms? He remembered with a quick breath the joy of his stolen kiss and the magical impact of her lips on his. His eyes searched each bedroom window, hoping for some sign of life. Oh, to catch a glimpse of her once again!

Billy reached for a flashlight stashed in the bedside table drawer. He lifted it to the window and switched it on and off at least a dozen times, but there was no response. As the night deepened, he saw the bedroom lights go out one by one, and he was left standing alone in the dark.

Darkness. Always darkness. Sometimes he could imagine light even in darkness, but occasionally, on a night such as this, it was dark on dark. He slipped out of his clothes and lay in his bed, miserable with desire. If only the girl had reappeared to him once again! If only she had signaled back in the darkness to him. If only he could be with her just for one night. If only Mother hadn't died and left him alone in this world!

He put away his flashlight and settled into his bed. Perhaps he had only dreamed of the girl on the shore. He turned away from the window, heartsick at such a black thought. He was not at all sure that the girl he so desperately loved was real, even though the ache in his heart was sharper now than ever before.

For some time he watched the flash of headlights from passing cars on the side street sweep across the ceiling of his room. He imagined they were comets shooting across the night sky and that he was far below them in the sea, lost on silver-crested waves.

CHAPTER 9

Pleasing Elizabeth

When Elizabeth was alive, Mary had been good to her, as had most all of her family, and given her much of her time. Often, she had ushered the children into the car and made the long trip to Chesapeake Avenue from her home on the Severn River in Gloucester to visit the woman they all called Aunt Elizabeth, the grand dame of the family, the matriarch, the one who held the family together.

Mary remembered her last visit with Elizabeth in her home. Elizabeth had been diagnosed earlier with breast cancer and had suffered the subsequent radical surgery in those days—removal of all breast tissue.

Aunt Elizabeth greeted them at the door. She was still in her nightdress but as on guard for imperfections as ever. "Tie your shoelace, Wake. Tuck in your shirt, Liz," she ordered even before greeting them. "You need a haircut, dear," she said to Mary, not unkindly. "You could stand to lose five pounds, too. Better do it now or you might regret it one day." The children busied themselves to correct their imperfections, but there was little Mary could do about her unruly hair and five extra pounds, which she was already regretting.

A few degrees more presentable now than before they had knocked on Elizabeth's door, they were led into the front parlor to sit on the twin green brocade horsehair loveseats to await iced tea, lemonade and cookies, which Veala delivered on a silver tray. The cookies were still warm from the oven, and Mary realized that Veala had made them just for their visit.

"Thank you, Veala," Mary said, treating herself to a cookie in spite of her five extra pounds. "They are quite delicious, as always. You really know how to spoil us."

"Have you met Robert, my dears?" Elizabeth asked the children after they had swallowed their cookies, emptied their drinks, and begun to fidget. Wake's foot had started to bang against the leg of the loveseat to the beat of some inward tune, indicating that he was on the verge of becoming rambunctious.

"Noooooo, we haven't met Robert," they answered, only slightly curious.

"Well, then, you must go upstairs, children. Robert is in the guest bedroom. He is studying for his exams in the morning. He is going to be a doctor. You may be doctors, too, one day! You must be very quiet so as not to disturb him!"

The children rushed to the staircase and, after the usual scramble to settle who would go first with the other tagging closely behind, they climbed the steps the rest of the way quietly. "Shhhh," Liz, who was in the lead, warned her little brother. "We mustn't disturb Robert!"

Elizabeth and Mary sat and sipped the cool tea. They heard the children creep from one bedroom to the next, opening and closing each door quietly. Soon they returned, clambering down the staircase, not worrying whom they disturbed. "We couldn't find Robert!" they announced in unison.

"Oh, that bad Robert!" cried Elizabeth, a frown deepening the creases on her forehead. "I should bet he has crept down the back stairway and gone out to play! That rapscallion! He knows he should be studying for his exams tomorrow. What an irresponsible boy! How will I ever fashion a doctor out of him?

"I often walked to the house for my lunch break when I worked at the hospital." Elizabeth vaguely continued her conversation with Mary while glancing out the window. "I would see Billy sitting there on the front porch, home from school on a break, his bare feet stretched out on the white banister as if he owned the place. He would be drinking beer. My own stepson! Drinking beer! On my front porch! Just steps away from the hospital! I never thought I would ever see such a day. Or live it down. Nor that he would make anything of himself."

Mary stared into her iced tea. What could she say? Aunt Elizabeth's stepson had just won the Pulitzer Prize for literature.

"At sixteen! Drinking beer on my front porch . . . " Elizabeth's voice trailed off. Veala appeared with more cookies and lemonade.

"I have read that William Faulkner walked around his town barefoot with a piece of straw in his mouth, a total wastrel, until he was thirty," Mary said brightly. "He went on to win the Nobel Prize for literature. One never knows about talent." But Elizabeth did not respond.

"Don't ever give up using linen napkins, dear. Paper napkins are a disgrace. No matter how times change, our kind of people must continue to observe some bare modicum of decency."

"Yes, Aunt Elizabeth." She awaited the next non sequitur that would fall like the blade of a guillotine.

"And don't plant trees in your yard. They only make mowing grass more difficult. It is becoming more expensive to hire lawn care. You and Chip may have to mow your own lawns in future years."

"Yes," replied Mary, who had just planted one thousand pine trees in the back acreage of her farm.

"And what about the children's christening? Isn't it time for them to be christened properly in the church? What do you intend to do about their christening, Mary? Time is passing!"

"Well . . . I haven't made any plans as yet, Aunt Elizabeth."

"But my dear, the family expects something. We hope for the Episcopal Church, of course, but any church is better for the children than no church!"

Mary sat dumbly, trying to think of some response.

"We could have it done in my church, St. Paul's. My priest would be charmed to christen my great-niece and -nephew in the same church where I was christened—along with every other member of the family."

"Well . . . " Mary thought of Elizabeth's cancer. "I suppose we could plan such an event for Liz, but Wake is too young. Would that please you, Aunt Elizabeth?"

"Oh! It would make me so very happy, my dear! In my last years! It would be like dotting my i's and crossing my t's. Making sure things were right for my very own namesake. Someone in the family has to be in charge of these things, God only knows."

Mary looked out the window at the far horizon. She saw the U.S. Navy ships berthed at the Norfolk naval base. The grey behemoths lay like whales at dock. She sighed. "All right, then; if the christening of Liz in your church would please you, Aunt Elizabeth, I'll agree to it."

"Then it's settled!" Elizabeth jumped up and raced to the phone. Mary had not seen such excitement from her ever before. She plucked up the phone and dialed a number she apparently knew by heart. "She's agreed to it! We have only to set a date! The last Sunday in the month?" She turned to Mary for a nod, which Mary gave immediately. "Perfect! I'll send her by directly with the children to sign the forms."

Elizabeth rushed back to Mary. Her cheeks were flushed, and she looked happier than Mary had ever seen her. "You must meet with my priest, the Reverend George Estes—he's such a fine man—just for a few minutes. It's only a formality, a few papers, that sort of thing. I shall have a big party for the family and friends afterwards at the James River Country Club! I must get my invitations out at once!

"This calls for a celebration!" she said, making her way to the dining room and getting out some glass tumblers. "May I offer you some sherry for a toast?" Mary held out her glass and she poured just a small amount. "To the new Episcopalian!" The children stared back at her and blinked. The women clinked glasses.

"Veala! Veala!" Elizabeth called, and the maid came rushing out from the kitchen. "I have wonderful news. My namesake will be christened at St. Paul's at the end of the month!"

"Why, that's such good news, Mrs. Styron!" Veala turned to Mary in a low voice. "What a kind thing to do for your aunt. I know how important this is for her. She's been talking about it since your daughter was born." This said, Veala disappeared back to the kitchen.

"Dr. Russell will be so happy!" Elizabeth continued, replacing the glasses on a silver tray. "I must call him immediately to tell him the good news." She placed an exuberant kiss on the forehead of each child. "And I shall tell Robert, too, when he comes back from his play. He shall be very happy, indeed!"

"Did Robert join up with the church too, Aunt Elizabeth?" asked Liz.

"No, Robert has nothing to do with the church. He is a non-believer and quite a bad little boy, actually."

Mary, realizing that her squirming children were ready to leave, rounded them up and headed for the door.

"Wait a minute, dear; we might as well talk about this now, depressing as it is. I want Russell's boys to have my three diamond rings; one for you, the others to Buck and Luke. You are to have my dinner ring, which was my mother's. It is to go down to your daughter . . . my namesake. My mother's silver cutlery will be yours, but not her tea service. That is to go to John, as he did not get anything at Papa's death. I want things to be fair. And you are to have this dining room chest. It came from dear Papa's house. And also, you can have the twin love sofas and the maple four poster twin beds."

"Thank you, Aunt Elizabeth. It is most kind of you to be thinking of us." Mary felt embarrassed as she headed out the door.

"I shall see to it that the three boys all get something from the big house. I have it all written down in my will, and Chip is to be my executor . . . so nobody can pull any shenanigans after my death," Elizabeth added, as if she believed someone was certainly bound to try to do so.

⌒

"What doesn't Robert believe, Mother?" the children asked when they were back in the car a few minutes later and heading for old St. Paul's in downtown

Newport News. There were a few rough neighborhoods to cross, and Mary leaned over to lock the car doors.

"Robert is just a pretend person. He's Aunt Elizabeth's pretend child."

"What's that?" asked Wake.

"Like when you are talking to an imaginary friend. He really isn't there. Only in your mind."

"Oh. But I didn't know grown-ups did that sort of thing," said Liz.

"Why can't I be Christianed too?" asked Wake, petulantly sticking out his lower lip.

"It's christened, dear. You're too young. Perhaps when you are your sister's age."

"It isn't fair!" complained Wake, kicking his foot against the car seat to register his protest.

Reverend Estes was waiting for them at the front door of the church when they pulled up to the curb. "You have made your aunt so very happy, Mary." He walked them through the church to his office, and the little group followed meekly. It was dark, but the many stained glass windows let in beams of colored light that flooded the ruby red rug leading to the altar. The priest stopped at the altar, bowed deeply, and turning abruptly left, marched into his office. Hesitating and then finally deciding not to emulate his bow, Mary and her children trailed after him. He did not look, but she somehow felt that he had noticed this omission and that she had already committed some grave sin.

Well, I am like a pagan, she thought, totally ignorant of religious practice and therefore not guilty of anything.

"Your religion, Mary?"

"Well, I went to Sunday school occasionally at the Congregational Church back in Vermilion, Ohio."

"Oh? Is that your parents' religion then?"

"No. Father is an atheist."

"I see. Would you like to take confirmation classes and also join the church? So that everyone in the family will eventually be of one church?" he added gently.

"Perhaps at a later date."

"Would you like your son christened with his sister?"

"Not at this time, thank you."

"As you wish, Mary. But, of course, the children are Buxtons. They should be raised in the family church. Given a proper religious background. Otherwise they will be rootless and unhappy all their lives."

"Yes, of course."

There was the matter of Mary assigning godparents, something she had never heard of except in childhood fairy tales, filling out forms, and finally signing them. It was over in minutes.

Driving back to Gloucester, with the children singing songs and bouncing in the back seat, Mary was filled with satisfaction. She felt as if she had done something good; she had given Aunt Elizabeth a measure of happiness simply by agreeing to her small request. It is good and right to give unto others what they want, and it took so little of me, she thought. After all, wasn't that what religion was supposed to do—help one to spread peace and happiness, starting with your own family, and then moving on to the rest of the world? It was the least she could do for Elizabeth while she was still in remission and feeling well. How proud she'll be at the christening! She will reign like a queen over her family, as she well should!

Mary smiled as she pictured Elizabeth holding court at St. Paul's Church, queen of her element, flushed with happiness that her namesake would follow in her footsteps—secure in her belief that all would be well for her offspring; and later again at the James River Country Club, perhaps stationed in front of the oil painting of King James himself, hosting her christening party for her nephew's young daughter with perfect charm and elegance.

"It was the Christian thing to do," Mary later told Chip over an evening cocktail. "Why not give happiness to others, if at all possible? It is so easy, after all."

CHAPTER 10

The Wake

Odd how he could still remember all the cutting remarks. She was a master at the craft of put-downs and insults, better than even the most sarcastic upperclassmen at Christchurch School. She had the uncanny ability to know everything about him even before he did, and he could still suffer at the mere memory of her every cut.

Just one subtle sweep of her all-seeing, pale blue gaze, and she could spot a sudden bulge in his pants, a trace of suspicious mud on the bottom of his shoes, a smudge of lipstick on his collar, bits of grass still clinging to the back of his tennis sweater, all suggesting ecstasy beyond her wildest imagination . . . Oh yes, he was guilty, alright. She was so adept at noticing his violation of any rule, any incriminating whiff of tobacco or alcohol on his breath, that there was no sense in lying to her. She always suspected the worst, and most of the time even he had to admit she was right on the money in her immediate judgment.

Headmaster Smith, although Sty knew he had a kind heart, could also mortify a teenager. At age fifteen, it was an obvious embarrassment for a boy not to excel at any team sport. But even worse than that, as Sty soon learned, was a boy not even giving a damn about sports. At prep school, participation in sports was everything. It was part of Southern manhood, even more important than academics. Without athletic prowess, a boy simply could not develop the competitive spirit that would help him become a captain of industry or a leader in his community. Nor would he learn cooperative skills that come from playing on a team—skills deemed necessary for one who wished to become a true bulwark in Southern society.

"Surely you could play some sport, young man?" Headmaster Smith had asked during an interview called shortly after the announcement that Sty had not made the school football team. Sty sat quite miserably in the leather chair opposite the headmaster's desk, searching for some slight interest in an activity that might suffice as a sport.

"I like chess."

"Chess? Not a chance, Sty. Contact sports, my boy, rough and tough baseball, football, basketball, wrestling, that sort of thing. You'll have to find a sport that you can play and play well if you mean to fit in here."

After failing to make the football team, Sty finally managed to make the junior varsity basketball team, where he stayed for the rest of his high school years. That saved him from the mortification of social rejection. He finally was seen as a regular boy, and he could have macho friends and not have to slink through his days on campus as if he had the plague, a chess player, a tennis freak, a weakling and a social flop.

Later, at the funeral wake at the James River Country Club, Bill spotted Mary in the throng. As they talked, he found himself speaking of his best friend at Christchurch, many years ago.

"Vincent, a fellow classmate who was also of a creative bent, became my soul mate. We spent every possible minute together. He later became the movie reviewer for the *New York Times*, and our friendship provided me with some desperately important artistic bonding," he said. "If you are a writer, Mary, you will need someone like that in your life too," he added.

Bill went on to explain how the two boys had somehow found each other in that macho, sport-crazed environment, and, as if each had immediately spotted the hidden artiste in the other, they had become instant best friends. Together they had explored each other's creative minds, and Bill had learned, at that early stage, what joy was to be found in intellectual bonding. They began writing satires of the faculty and publishing their stories in the school newspaper. They lived just to write the next amusing piece.

"Did you have an idea at that time that you were going to become a novelist?" Mary asked in the rising sea of surrounding conversations. She now had to raise her voice to be heard.

"Hell, no. I just enjoyed writing. It was pretty bad stuff, my high school writing. But it got me through that first year. We used to write spoofs of all the campus events, and we especially enjoyed lampooning the faculty. I was in a play, too, that first year. I really liked being in the play. And I liked the poetry in English classes. I remember reading a poem at graduation, 'Gunga Din,' and I hammed it up with my best effort at a Cockney accent, too. It made my father proud. I always loved anything associated with the arts. I took all my English classes in Bishop Brown, second floor. I remember sitting at my desk, looking out the window, and wondering about all the stuff we were reading, trying to make sense of it as to how any of it related to my life. The classics, all the poetry, I liked it all. That might have told me something about my future in itself, because the usual boy at prep school is not that much interested in literature classes." Bill laughed at the memories, but Mary took in every word as if God himself were speaking to her.

"There you are, Billy Styron! I want to talk to you!" came the shrill cry of a stout, elderly woman pushing her way through the crowd. "I know that you based that dreadful Helen Loftis in your first book on Elizabeth! It was obvious. Shameful! I know she knew it, too, and it deeply hurt her, although she never spoke of it. She tried her best to be a good mother to you, and how did you treat her, Billy Styron? How? I'll tell you how! You drove her half crazy with your constant disrespect and rebellion!"

Bill turned abruptly to the woman, gave a curt half-smile and a mock bow, and left the room. "You were a traitor to your family and friends in Newport News!" the woman called after him. Mary hoped that Bill had not heard the last of her comments. She watched his solemn figure as he wound his way out of the tightly knit groups and exited at the front door, bent over like a tragic figure in a Shakespearean play.

He must have circled the country club via the golf clubhouse entrance, because Mary soon caught sight of him walking alone along the shore of the James River. He was stooped over in the growing dusk, still carrying his drink, and gazing out at the muddy river, the wide horizons, as if he were trying to find the consoling company of a stray ship or barge steaming downriver to the sea. But little ship activity passed the country club, which was positioned too far up the James River for one to see any commercial ships passing.

"Billy went to elementary school at Hilton, just around the corner," the woman continued telling Mary. "I knew his mother. She was a lovely woman. Died of cancer, she did. A long and painful death. Strangely enough, the same cancer took Elizabeth. The poor woman—marrying late in life and suddenly finding herself saddled with that rebellious upstart of a kid who broke every rule of decency and resisted every principle she believed in. She had a time raising that young man, I can tell you. She could never please him, no matter what she did. I don't know how she survived those years. We were in the garden club together. I heard of all the dissension firsthand, you might say. It was a blessing he was off in prep school or college most of the time, I can tell you that. Even so, the weekend visits and summers took their toll. No woman deserved a stepson like that!"

"Excuse me; I don't believe I have met you," Mary said to the older woman. "I'm Chip Buxton's wife, Mary."

"Oh. You're from Ohio."

"Yes."

"Well, for goodness' sake; imagine Chippy growing up and having a wife. I was a friend of Elizabeth's. My sister was a Buxton nurse. That was the highest order in the profession in those days. She often talked about Chippy and his two brothers, Russell and Luke, as Red dropped them off at the hospital every time they went out of town, which was often, or so I've been told, and the nurses had to babysit the boys. Those boys ran all over the hospital."

Mary smiled politely. "Getting back to Bill, I really don't think it fair to label him a traitor because of *Lie Down in Darkness*."

"Well, he was a traitor! Pretended he was one of us! Well, he was one of us. No matter what he says now, Billy Styron was one of us. A Virginian right down to his toes. Not one bit better than us, either! Then he stormed off to New York City, told everyone he was going to be a writer—got deathly sick with all his wild parties, too. Elizabeth said he drank too much and never ate a decent meal. Almost died of hepatitis. Nothing Elizabeth or even his father could do could save him from his evil ways. And then he turned on us! Rose up from his deathbed and wrote a book about us. As if we were all demons. It was shameful! Especially the way he portrayed his loving stepmother. No woman deserved to be treated like that!" The woman had become flushed as she spoke, obviously worked up in her defense of the natives.

"He wrote about life in Tidewater as he saw it," Mary said calmly. "That's what writers do. Bill has a kind and tender heart, but he still saw the dark side of humanity and he described it well. Without writers, we would never see beyond the superficial in our lives. Like that saying, 'We wouldn't see the forest for the trees.'"

"Well, don't you have a high regard for yourself! Like most Yankees! You come down here from your home in the North and start preaching to the rest of us, as if you think you're better than us!"

"Not at all." Mary tried to remain calm, and her voice never changed in pitch, but she had turned a deep red, a sudden, high, indignant color, as if paint had spilled on her head and spread to her face, neck, and pale arms. "Bill wasn't writing about Tidewater in particular. Writers see all human behavior as universal. What Bill portrayed in his book is behavior everywhere. The dark side of human nature is in everyone, and no one is immune. Behavior here is no different than anywhere else in the world. Including Ohio," she added, still feeling angry.

The woman moved away, no longer interested in anything Mary had to say, and Mary realized the woman had never given her name. How silly it was, she decided, to be ruffled by someone you didn't even know, merely a stranger in the crowd.

"Excuse me, are you Mary Buxton?" another woman said as she moved close to her. "I'm Elsie Duval. I was a very close friend of Bill's family. And your family, too. We're related if you go back far enough. Are you Chippy's wife? I understand you're from Ohio?"

Mary had to shout her affirmative response. The crowd, exulting in their own company, almost surging together shoulder to shoulder, was now well into their drink. They were feeling better; the funeral was now behind them, and the grief at the loss of their good friend was beginning to wane.

"I knew Billy and his mother, and I was very close to Elizabeth," Elsie continued. "Did you read his first book, *Lie Down in Darkness*? You know, everyone in Newport News was furious when that book came out. Of course, he had changed all the names, but we knew Peyton was based on the suicide tragedy of one of our dearest friends. The family was deeply hurt by Bill's portrayal. And, of course, there was that dreadful mother figure, the weak-kneed father, the crippled sister, and this very James River Country Club; we all knew who they were and recognized the settings. What a wonderful writer he is! But many old Newport News families have never forgiven him. And never will," she added gently.

Mary sighed. She liked Elsie Duval, but she could see there would be no end to bearing the cross for her hero. "Bill captured the dark side of Virginia society in the times in which he set his novel. The blatant bigotry, that was all in the book, too. And the alcoholism . . . " Her voice trailed off, for she feared offending the pleasant woman. Her small-town Ohio upbringing had not prepared her for the whiskey-laced parties in Tidewater, where almost everyone drank alcohol as if it were water and politeness eventually collapsed, leaving people to say whatever they wished. The old adage was true, that wine certainly unloosed even the most courteous tongue.

"I've always been so very proud of Billy," Elsie continued. "Every writer must go aground with the locals when they actually read what the writer has written about them, especially if the writer has as much talent to identify human weaknesses as Billy did."

Mary glanced out the window and could still spot the solitary figure of

Bill on the shore. She suddenly excused herself from Elsie and slipped out a side door that led outside to the pool and beach beyond. It was dark now, and a full moon had risen from the black river. The James River Country Club was ablaze in lights, and the people within appeared to her as bobbing silhouettes in the long sweep of glass window that faced the river as she made her way to the beach. She thought, looking back at the country club, that it looked like a mammoth cruise ship lit up in the night.

Bill was seated on a log in the distance, his head in his hands and the sorry remains of his drink propped up in the sand. Mary hurried toward him, noting his hunched figure, his folded hands, his deep posture of despair.

She sat down next to him, picked up a stick, and drew a series of small circles in the sand. The sand was perfect for drawing images: firm, moist, with the receding tide leaving a smooth slate for her artwork. Huge dark clouds whisked by overhead, caught up in the fury of some planetary race, and the moon had come up from behind the trees on the opposite bank and lay low in the sky, like a silvery ball tossed up from the horizon. Waves lapped lazily on the beach, and Mary thought the low tide smelled exactly like her first breakfast of shad roe at her in-laws' residence at Christopher Shores.

"I'm having those black nightmares again," Bill said, beginning to ramble. "Crying out in the night, tossing, turning. Nightmares filled with fury and hate. Hatred is a good muse, you know. You should know that if you are going to be a writer, Mary. I hope to God you hate something so much that your work will be powered with its very fine edge: fresh, original, hard-hitting venom."

Mary said nothing.

"Then the darkness sets in, of course, as it is bound to do, like a fog turning everything slate grey. It always does," Bill continued. "It finally shuts down the creative brain and one gives in to the despair.

"I write everything on a yellow legal pad, Mary, did you know that? Everything in pencil. I never typed a word. Do you know how many times a writer has to sharpen his pencil if he is writing an entire novel in pencil?"

Mary still said nothing. This was listening time, not talking time, and she wanted to hear every word he said and remember it.

"You see, Mary, I saw only the dark side of people in Newport News, never the bright side. I never saw anything good about Elizabeth. Perhaps I should have given her more credit . . . after all, she was a pioneering woman in her times. At least when it came to her work at the hospital. But I was so consumed with the hatred I felt for her values, lifestyle, prejudices—and especially the way she had treated me as a child, trying to manipulate my every move . . . all else paled."

Bill stopped to reflect on what he had said. "And the hospital has always taken black patients, even when other hospitals built at a later time on the Peninsula refused to take the blacks. Did you know that, Mary? That Peninsula hospitals once refused to take Negro patients, that at one time in Virginia it was against the law for public facilities to integrate races? Now what do you have to say about that?"

"I didn't know that. I'm really proud to hear my family did that."

"Well, the hospital was private. They didn't have to follow the law."

Bill sank once again into silence. Mary did not move. She even tried to regulate her breathing, for fear the sound might disturb him.

"Yet she could not stand offering her hand to my dear friend, James Baldwin, when he stood with me at her front door. Imagine that, Mary! She could not stand that, a black man, an esteemed author, greeting her as an equal. How dare she insult him!

"I despised her," he mumbled into the dregs of his drink, now recovered from its sand perch. As she watched him try to find a few more drops of golden liquid in his glass, she knew they would soon be returning to the party, if only to get refills on bourbon.

"Nobody likes their stepmother, Bill, especially at fifteen years of age. You just have to understand that and get over it." Mary flushed in the dark. She was instantly embarrassed at what she had said. Her advice sounded so naïve. She felt like a child.

Yet the night had taken on a magical essence. To Mary, the euphoria she felt was not just the result of shared conversation between two friends, or the moon and stars that shone down from above, casting a silvery finish on the beach, or the flash of fish just under the surface of the ebony water. It was triggered by something much more profound—the hope, perhaps, of finally grasping some piece of previously misunderstood truth.

"Get over it," he repeated with a sigh. Mary again was horrified at hearing him repeat her shallow words.

"Well—" She took a deep breath and tried once again, hoping not to sound like a schoolgirl. "I think you just have to eventually understand there is a natural hostility between stepmothers and stepsons. They are both competing for the same prize."

"It's much more, Mary. It's a hellish duty we writers must shoulder. We must write what we see, what we feel, what we know to be truth. Whether it is beautiful or not, whether it will be received kindly or not. Whether we will be able to sell our work or not. Whether it will make us popular or not. None of these other things matter. Yet we must write or, throttled, die in despair!"

"What if what I see and what you see is different? Which one of us is telling the truth?" Mary asked.

"We both tell the truth! Truth is universal but also individualistic. Yet my truth is just as relevant as your truth. Precious pieces of the puzzle. And the entire world depends on us and our ability to hear and see and record our versions of the truth. We must write in freedom and total individuality and with ongoing tolerance to hear each other!"

"But what about the social punishment that we must take when we write what we see? What about that? I'm already feeling some of it, when my family reads some of my work. Sometimes they don't like what I write. What am I to do about that?"

"You have every right to write about the world the way you see it!"

More silence. "I've received some angry letters from the family," Mary added in a hushed tone, as if unleashing some deep, dark secret.

He laughed, a shocking, raucous sound that cut through the evening's serenity. "Well, guess what, Mary? I've received some of those letters myself! And not just from angry members of the family. After *Confessions of Nat Turner*, most of the black writers turned against me. I had sold the movie rights and the black actors that were hired even refused to play their parts! They objected to my use of African-American dialect for my black characters in my book, of all things, but worse, they charged me with using black inflammatory stereotypes. The final blow was their claim that a white man could never tell a black man's story!"

Silence filled the air, and Mary breathed in the smell of the night, the sea, the earthy fragrance of the beach at low tide, the sweet smell of pine and bayberry that grew wild along the marshes.

"The same thing happened after *Sophie's Choice*. A Jewish writer asked me what business I had writing a story about a Jewish woman in a German concentration camp." Bill mumbled curse words under his breath.

They sat in silence looking at the river. Little lights twinkled across the river from the far shore in Smithfield.

"Could a woman writer dare to get into the mind of a male writer? Could a woman tell a man's story?"

"Any writer can tell anyone's story!" Bill cried out in anguish. "Our stories are human, universal, and they cancel membership in any gender, race, or religion! We all have a right to take a crack at the world and relate the truth that we see! That is our fundamental right!" he repeated, his throat becoming hoarse.

Bill took Mary's hand, as if to check whether she felt the same passion he did. She felt the power of his sentiment surge through her hand and into her body and brain like some mysterious electrical current. She imagined it as the physical imprint of his words. "I know I have to forgive them all before I can get well."

"Get well, Bill?"

"The black dog. Depression. You probably know nothing of that. You're too young. But it has tailed me throughout my life. It is the worst of all human ailments, for it alone has the power to stop my pen. When I am in the grips of the black dog, there is no writing, only darkness.

"My doctor tells me I must start coming back home to the Tidewater again on a regular basis," he continued. "Confront what it was about my home that I so despised, that which nearly drove me mad, until I could write the fury out of my burning brain. And, in the end, he believes this simple act of the return of the native will heal me."

"One hears that forgiveness is the best balm there is for whatever ails us."

"Forgiveness is sometimes not possible." He made a move upward and fell back to the log with a sudden thud. Mary offered him her arm, and they slowly rose upright together and headed for the glittering ship, a pair of tottering scribblers, unsteady from drink and walking in the sand, brave searchers of truth. Looking upon the bright crown of lights shining down on the beach from the country club, the twinkling gems of each window, and the black forms moving along the long span of glass, Mary felt deeply thrilled. It seemed to her that they were all part of some great play being presented on an evening stage, and that she had been given her cue to begin reciting her lines.

"They will be looking for us," he said as they made the ascent to the clubhouse. They could hear the babble of hundreds of conversations as they reentered the door and met with spouses who were more than ready to leave, Bill heading back with his father and Rose for one more night at his old boyhood home on Chesapeake Avenue, Mary returning to her home on the Severn River in Gloucester.

Chapter 11

Bidding Farewell

Just days before Aunt Elizabeth's funeral, Chip pulled into the parking lot next to the hospital that overlooked the water. It was a stifling hot day, and it seemed to Chip that steam was rising off the water. He could see Navy ships moving in and out of port as he walked from his car to the lobby, and the view was so exhilarating he could barely take his eyes away from the water and concentrate on the dire business at hand.

Hundreds of times he had made such a trip to the hospital, first as a young boy to see his father or to be left under the oversight of the nurses when his parents went out of town, and then as a young man to check on friends or members of his own ailing family. He returned again much later, as an attorney, to check on a client who needed sickbed assistance with some pressing legal matter. Seeing the hulks of the grey ships in the water nearby made him melancholy. He remembered his years in the Navy during the Vietnam War and thought of the constant movement of ships. He felt, as the dutiful son and nephew making his many visits to the hospital to care for aging relatives—all of whom seemed to end up in the same room—that he was like the vessels, moving in and out of the harbor.

Chip entered the lobby, which had hardly changed since his grandfather, grandmother, father, and aunt had been in charge. The Bernadine Sisters, a Catholic order of nuns from Philadelphia, had purchased the hospital in 1954, and Chip saw that a portrait of the Pope now hung in the lobby, rather than the elegant oil paintings of his grandparents and father that had once graced those walls.

Chip smiled at the memory of another change. The classic Buxton nurse's uniform had given way to more practical wash-and-wear material, much to the chagrin of the original nurses who thought the new look common. The starched white blouses and pleated skirts that had been so difficult to maintain had been replaced by simple polyester uniforms. The perky cap with the RN pin affixed in exactly the correct location, along with the smart navy blue and red-lined cape with the old hospital logo sewn across the front, were now mere charming memories. The nurses today looked identical to the nurses in all the other area hospitals. The old, proud esprit de corps of the family hospital had gone with the capes.

But the marriage between the family and Catholic nuns had been a good one. As Chip stepped into the elevator that would take him up to the third floor, he saw that the hospital was still kept in immaculate condition both inside and out, just as it had been when his family owned it.

But now Elizabeth was dying. Earlier in the morning, when Chip had been working in his corporate office at the shipyard, Uncle Bill had called him from his wife's hospital bedside. "Not good here, Chip," he had whispered over the phone, obviously trying to shield his conversation from Elizabeth. "You had better get over here as soon as you can if you want to bid farewell. This morning, if possible," he added. "I don't think she will last much longer." Chip had immediately set aside his paperwork and headed for his car.

The elevator opened to the third floor, which was reserved for the seriously ill and dying. The corridors had been freshly waxed and gleamed in the fluorescent overhead light. Most of the nurses scurrying up and down the hallway were Bernadine sisters, but Chip could still spot an occasional Buxton nurse. He saw them all dressed in their white gowns and caps or, if they were nuns, matching white veils, and he thought they looked like angels as they breezed by him, their feet barely touching the floor.

Chip remembered the many times when his parents had gone out of town for the day and deposited him and his two brothers to be cared for by the nurses at the hospital. He remembered his favorite forms of amusement:

riding up and down the elevators, pushing laundry carts filled with clean sheets back and forth down the hallways, and delivering trays of food to the patients in order to "help" the nurses. He laughed out loud to himself at the memories. Many years later, a few of the nurses had confided in him that the three Buxton boys had been holy terrors in the corridors, hardly more than spoiled brats. But the nurses, always good sports, would never have complained that they had been stuck looking after the devilish boys when the boss was away.

Chip walked to Elizabeth's room at the end of the hall—the VIP room, the one that faced the water. Elizabeth was on everyone's minds this morning, and as soon as Chip saw her, he knew the end was near. Every member of the staff, including the landscape help and delivery crew, was painfully aware that a long-time hospital icon was passing on. Not since the death of Dr. Joseph in 1941 had there been such a royal, in-house passing.

She had been hooked up to every piece of the latest equipment in medical life-saving technology possible, as if one more plastic tube might spare her from death for one more day. Bill slumped in a chair pulled close to her bed and held Elizabeth's pale hand. There was no movement from her, but Chip could hear a faint rasp of breath.

"Elizabeth," Bill called to her. "Chip's here to be with you, dearest." She gave no answer beyond a distant tiny sound, like the mew of a kitten. It was enough response, however, and Chip knew that she was aware of his presence.

"Thank you for coming," Uncle Bill said simply. "Russell and Virginia are out of town. It seemed only right that someone from the family be here with her this morning." Bill broke down and wept silently into a white handkerchief that he clutched in his gnarled, blue-veined hands, his heaving shoulders the only indication of his grief.

"I'm here, Aunt Elizabeth," Chip said, walking to the bed and putting his hand around his uncle's shoulder. He lightly touched his fingers to her ashen cheek. "We're making sure that all is in order." He knew such words would probably be of the greatest comfort to her in such circumstances. What more could he say, he wondered. What more can one say as one's family member faces the end?

The tiniest sound emanated from the woman, just sixty-nine years old, who had led the hospital nursing school for so many years after her mother had passed away. She had held the rambunctious next generation of the family together as best she could, though poignantly disappointed that not one of Dr. Russell's three boys would follow in the family footsteps.

Chip struggled to think of something to say. He spoke of all the good things she had done for him and his family over the years: the times she had taken in the boys; the parties she had hosted for graduations, regattas, or birthdays, and even his own engagement party. She seemed to hear and understand his last words of appreciation.

When Chip could think of nothing more to say, he looked up helplessly to Uncle Bill and was relieved to see that Reverend Estes from St. Paul's Church, Elizabeth's beloved rector, had joined them to say final prayers. Never had he been so happy to see a priest in his life, for he had run out of words. She was gone by lunchtime.

In the end, some of the old Buxton nurses whom she had taught over the years had come to the hospital and quietly surrounded her bed in one large circle. They were joined by the Bernadine sisters who were on duty that day. The nurses had noiselessly crept into the room one by one, as had several physicians, and had formed a second and third ring of medical personnel all dressed in white. It was an appropriate and fitting farewell to one of their own, and she would have approved.

Within minutes of Elizabeth's death, Bill Styron had his son in Connecticut on the phone. "She's gone, Billy," he had said, weeping into the phone.

After promising his father that he would fly down for the funeral planned on Saturday, the son hung up the phone and thought of his own mother. She had been dying the summer he had turned fourteen, back in 1939. Hitler had moved into Poland and Europe was on the brink of another world war. He had gone out to deliver the newspapers that morning, just as he had always done each morning that year, and he remembered reading the front page, which was covered with the mounting bad news of impending war. Then, that one unforgettable morning, when he had returned home from his work, she was gone. He had walked into the house and found his father standing at her bedside weeping. Just like that, his mother was gone.

Bill realized that he hadn't even said good-bye to her when he had taken off that morning to deliver his papers, just as the sun was coming up in the eastern sky. He hadn't even said good-bye.

One died at home in those days, Bill thought, as he stared at the telephone in his home in Connecticut. The family was with you through the worst of it. Bill thought that such a death, back then, had been better than how people died today, off somewhere in an antiseptic white room, in the wee hours of the morning, far away from family members cozily tucked in their beds, exhausted from the day's vigil at the hospital. The last thoughts of such family members before they turned over to fall asleep were probably worries over whether their loved one would die in the night. Now beloved family members, diapered with the latest no-stain fabrics and doped up with morphine, were surrounded by strangers—nurses and staff members, even the orderly, wheeling out the last batch of urine-stained sheets to the laundry, as some poor soul took his last breath.

Cancer kills slowly. Better to drink yourself to death, he thought. Alcohol, morphine, pain pills; who really cares what it is as long as it numbs the horror of reality? Leaves a man mumbling nonsense. In the end it is all babbling, isn't it? Girlfriends, neighbors, old classmates. Whatever. No sleep. Just fading into unconsciousness and hoping to check out as fast as possible into the awaiting, perpetual darkness.

CHAPTER 12

Living Memories

Memories, Bill thought, as he hung up the receiver after speaking to his father. They keep coming back to a man again and again as if they had a life of their own. They never die so long as a poor soul can still breathe.

Bill could still hear his own mother's cries in the night. He remembered how he would lie in his childhood bed in Hilton with pillows over his head, as if anything could ever muffle those ghastly sounds. No one had to tell him she was in unbearable pain. Cries in the night can carry through the house and leave a sound in a young boy's ears that can never be erased.

But how she had smiled! She had always smiled! Sitting in her chair, her beautiful white hair combed perfectly, the lilt of lemon scent in the air, the afternoon sun streaming through the windows . . . oh, how he ached at the memories. Even at the end, she had smiled at him and looked so serene.

He thought his mother might have known that he would become a writer. His father had always told him that he was like her in the way that he saw life. A different spin, a new slant; he would be interesting to read. Such traits stand out in a child: being slightly off course, the curiosity at the sudden storm, the obsessive anticipation of the coming jibe. Such attributes are easy to spot in children but far more difficult to pick up on in adults, who have long learned the tricks of protecting their true nonconforming natures.

That woman thought she could deny my genes—turn me into a doctor, lawyer, or engineer! he thought bitterly. "Writers are no better than actors," she had told him many times. "You have to become something respectable,

Billy. You have to support yourself. Writers can't possibly earn a decent living. Your parents will not be paying your bills forever, you know. One day you will have to get a job and earn your own keep. No wonder your mother died, the way you must have kept worrying her. The way you have treated me. Resisting every sensible plan I have ever suggested, fighting me at every turn of the screw. No wonder that poor woman died! You'll end up being the death of me, too, Billy. Yes, I believe you will!"

"Now, Elizabeth," his father would intercede if he had happened to hear such wounding words. "Now, Elizabeth; now, Elizabeth," anything to stop that ongoing stream of spewed degradation and judgment. "Let the boy become what he wants to become in life."

Bill thought of his stepmother and tried to remember good memories. A summer conversation with a neighbor and friend, Elsie Duval, came to mind: "Your stepmother called me yesterday, Billy. She said you wanted to become a writer."

He had been seventeen when he had bumped into Elsie at the corner drugstore. She had told him that she had just returned from a writer's conference at Middlebury College in Vermont. "Robert Frost himself read my work and advised me! You ought to go to that same camp next summer, Billy. It did me a lot of good with my writing."

Robert Frost! That name was all he could think of all year long. He had begged his family to send him to the same camp so he could learn to write, too. Billy had gone to the camp the very next summer, and it was Elizabeth who had paid the tuition. Elsie had reported the glowing follow-up call from Elizabeth right after he had returned home. "Oh, Elsie, Billy had a wonderful time at camp!" she had raved over the phone. "He wanted to bring all the writers he met up North home to Virginia with him. He really identified with those people, Elsie. He felt he was with his own kind. Can you imagine such a thing? Writers, of all things! I had hoped the camp would finally drive all thoughts about making writing a life's profession out of his system once and for all. But now I do believe he really wants to become a writer. Oh, but how will he pay his bills, Elsie? How will he support a family? We can't support him the rest of his life, Elsie!"

That endearing memory of Elizabeth's generosity in sending him off to Vermont was short-lived, and his thoughts again turned dark. He could hear her voice ranting on and on: "Those writers! Those obnoxious, horrifying people! Those silly, time-wasting scribblers! The lowest scum of the earth! The sorts who live off their parents their entire lives, like parasites attached to the flesh of another animal, and shirk all duty to their families and society!"

To Elizabeth, Bill thought grimly, writers were hardly better than that. They were the filthy and the unmannered of this world, the unstructured, lazy, unemployed, and unprincipled. A sleazy and suspicious lot, perhaps tolerated in society, but certainly not what one would hope for in one's very own family.

Bill recalled how he finally had given up trying to become a writer at home. After college and a short stint in the marines, he had taken off for New York City, determined at last to cast his lot with the creative thinkers of this world. He connected with people who became famous in the arts—writers, poets, and playwrights—and Bill knew Elizabeth would have been shocked at his friends. Most of them went on to become well known and respected in their fields: Mike Wallace, Art Buchwald, and James Baldwin, just to name a few.

Bill's thoughts raced as he recalled the time he had come home to Virginia to do research for *The Confessions of Nat Turner*. He had brought James Baldwin home to her house for supper.

"Oh, Elsie!" Elizabeth ranted within his earshot, in near hysteria, the next day. "He called me to say he was coming home for dinner and that he would be bringing a friend. I set the table for four, Elsie. And his friend was black! Black, Elsie! Black as the ace of spades! Some writer Billy had said he was working with on research for his new novel. That was one of his best friends. Can you imagine that, Elsie? Not even to be considerate enough to tell his parents that his friend was black? Can you imagine doing something like that to your very own parents? The shock of it all! To open the door and see this black man, tall, well dressed, well educated, standing there, smiling at me with all those white teeth, expecting to shake my hand. To call me by my first name! Can you imagine such a thing, Elsie? Why, I almost went into cardiac arrest, right at my own front door, not to mention how his poor father felt!"

Bill smiled at the delight of it all, in spite of the bitterness he still felt at the memory all these years later. But other memories returned to erase his sudden merriment. After his mother had died, Bill remembered, his father had sunk into deep depression. It was as if he'd just checked out of life, leaving his young son standing there, looking at him sprawled across his mother's bed and weeping like a child. There was nothing Billy could do for his father. Friends came, he remembered. His father had to be hospitalized, indeed, went to the Buxton hospital to recover, and there was Elizabeth, who nursed him back to health. She had been so consumed with her nursing work that she had never dated a man in her life, and there Father had landed, right in her net. Flattered by all the attention, treated like a big shot at the hospital—she had even seen to it that he was assigned the VIP room—he realized this was an opportunity he'd never had before in his life. He could "marry up" in the world, as he called it, into a Virginia family that would make a Tar Heel proud. Everyone was shocked at the budding romance, especially Mother's old friends—they were flabbergasted. Even Elizabeth's family had been surprised at the turn of events.

Billy was soon sent off to prep school. He knew, in spite of what his father said, that Elizabeth had wanted him out of the way. She'd said it was good to meet a better caliber of people than the usual motley crowd he ran with on the streets. That constant, demeaning judgment of his old Hilton friends had first triggered his hatred for that woman.

She's dead now. Bill stood and stared out his farmhouse window at the New England woods, but saw in the horizon of his mind the remembered beaches of Hilton that he had known so well as a boy, growing up in that house on the corner. The stretches of sand were wild and undeveloped then;

a boy could run all day long and try to forget a mother moaning in the night, three walls and a staircase away, but so loudly that not even two pillows over his head could erase the sounds.

CHAPTER 13

The House in Warwick

One morning Bill drove over to his childhood home in Warwick, now called Hilton Village, where he had lived before his father married Elizabeth. Parking his rental car under one of the neighborhood's large, lush shade trees—perhaps the very one where a neighbor's son had fashioned a swing they had used throughout their youth—he walked down the street to the corner house.

He felt himself trembling as he approached the modest, white-framed house. In his mind's eye, he saw his mother standing at the front door, smiling—she had such a lovely smile—then waving to him, beckoning him to come in and wash up for dinner. He saw his father as a young man, home for lunch from the shipyard and sitting in the swing on the front porch reading the newspaper. He saw a little boy, one shoe off, one shoe on, playing with his dog in the yard, and realized that boy was himself.

A couple of dirt bikes now leaned against the front porch and a baseball glove and bat lay on the front steps. It was obvious to Bill that a family with young children, probably a couple of boys, still lived in the old home, and he was glad of it. It was a good house for a boy to grow up in, a boy who had his real mother to take care of him, and not some trumped-up stepmother married into the family in order to afford a depressed father some much-craved society in his later years.

The house had been close to the old Hilton School, and he used to walk down the street a few blocks to his classrooms. There were no worries in those days about weird people who might snatch a child away.

Then there was the James River. In his youth it was mainly undeveloped, with wild and wonderful beaches that ran up and down the shoreline, lending a curious boy room to explore and experience real adventure. If nothing particularly exciting happened during the day at school, a boy with a creative brain and an isolated beach could always imagine some adventure. The beach had a pier jutting out into the river, from which one could swim or fish or observe sunrises and sunsets, and where one could just stand and weep for happiness at the great, big, beautiful world. How many full moons had he seen there as a boy, and how many stars had he counted there in the night? And if that hadn't been enough inspiration for his imagination, there had always been Navy warships going out to sea to battle the Germans, or airplanes flying overhead. Warwick back then when his mother was alive was a perfect place to grow up, a place for knowing the plain joy of life, where the days passed one after another without one whiff of trouble and the river ever stretched to far horizons.

His eyes traveled to the front upstairs window. He could imagine his mother lying in bed in her white lace nightclothes. He could see her hair, streaked with grey, flowing out from the propped pillows like wisps of clouds on a summer day. "Please get me some water, Billy," she asked, in a voice so faint he could hardly make out the words.

It was hot, like all Tidewater days in the summer, and there was nothing in those days to offer cooling but a fan that whirred lazily on the ceiling. He filled her glass with water from the bedside pitcher and turned and left the house, slamming the back screen door behind him. The boy couldn't wait to get away, to spend the day laughing and talking to friends or exploring on his own—anything to escape doing chores around the house or sitting next to his sick mother and trying to think of something cheerful to say.

Bill thought he must have guessed that she was dying. Deep down, he must have known it, as much as any fourteen-year-old kid ever knows a parent will die one day and leave him alone in this world. Yet it would be months before she died, and with the beach calling him every day after school to some thrilling adventure, he could never seem to bear staying very long in her sickroom.

Bill walked down to the river and saw the old dock that he had used as the location for his character Peyton's suicide in *Lie Down in Darkness*. He had sat for hours at the end of this very same pier with a fishing pole, waiting for the day's big catch. If he got really lucky, he would land a flounder to take home for his mother to fry for dinner. But mostly he caught croaker, and spot, and occasional blow toads that were difficult to disengage from his hook to throw back into the sea. Then in the fall when the blues would run, he would go with a friend on the river in a boat and pull in fish by the dozens. The many hours spent waiting on the dock for a strike or just watching passing boats or studying patterns in the river and sky could probably have made up a year of his life. He had never dreamed that, one day, someone would use this idyllic site to bring an end to life, or that he would later write of the incident.

I didn't know about suicide in those days, Bill thought. Nor darkness. Nor depression. But he had liked to watch a storm form in the west and come tearing downriver, with an armada of black clouds and wind so strong it turned the mirrored water into whitecaps in seconds and sent the pine trees leaning hard over, as if in prayer. He imagined that the urge to escape a troubled life by suicide was just as powerful in the mind as a storm on the river.

Nobody knows what it is like to be a writer, Bill thought. There is no more isolated or lonely profession on this earth. Oh sure, they read our books and they chat us up at cocktail parties, and they purse their lips in deep thought over our efforts. "Do you like Bill's books?" they ask over a dinner gathering, and the other might or might not have read the books and understood the themes. And the writer might be the center of attention for a few minutes at the most respectable tables in town while they grapple over what in the world he is talking about in his strange portrayals of them. But they don't ever really understand him.

They think we're nuts, it suddenly occurred to Bill. "Weird" maybe is the word. "This stuff is weird," was what he would hear from more conventional minds. How the instant rejection hurt. But later he would come to realize the "This is weird" response was typical of the judgment of the common herd, and Elizabeth and her ilk would always be present to direct that chorus of voices against them. Then Bill smiled to himself. He knew the simple truth was that any writer who was ever able to capture some segment of truth in life was, indeed, a little wild and weird.

He was not at all sure at times that he wasn't crazy. One day he went for a walk at the farm back home in Roxbury. That day the wild geese flying south had passed directly overhead, and he had heard, suddenly, with no warning, that shrill cacophony of honk and gaggle. It had caused goose bumps to race up his arms and made his blood churn. He'd thought the sound must be exactly like the bedlam of an insane asylum. It had struck him then that this terrifying noise was the beginning and end of all reality. He had stopped in his tracks and stood perfectly still, staring after the geese, his mouth agape. Trembling, until the last of the flowing, unruly skein had passed by, he had suddenly known without doubt that he was insane. It had taken a close overhead encounter with Canadian geese to make him see this truth, which no doctor could possibly have managed, no matter how many psychiatric tests were thrown his way. No results could have convinced him of this diagnosis more than his reaction to wild geese.

In the end, it is obsession that grips the brain. It is some small detail of horror, some tiny human flaw in the universal pot that is magnified and swirled about over and over again in the misty gyre of the brain. A writer sees the human failing and can't forget it. The flaw troubles him, until finally it possesses him and destroys him. The very same stuff that no one else would even notice, let alone have the least response to, finally drives the writer to his pen.

The obsession grows. It cannot be dismissed or done with; it takes root in the very heart and soul of a man. He has to carry it wherever he goes and tell the world of what outrage he has known and the horror of it all. Great novels are made of such stuff.

A day of reckoning comes. He had seen this to be true in himself and others who finally, exhausted, turn to the balm of the bottle, which offers some release; but in time it also robs the pen of all brain and energy. In the end, perhaps there is nothing left to face the outrage but darkness and silence.

Bill left the James River and returned to his old house. He thought of knocking at the door and asking the new owners if he could walk through the house, but then decided against it. He took in one more sweep of vision from the past, of the heartbreak that so tore apart his young life. One last look—the final feast that would have to last the rest of his life, for he did not expect to ever return.

I am at my peak now, Bill thought, the top of my line. Exciting; even now, words gushed forth from his brain like water from a primed pump in a backyard well. A man can't write fast enough to release the inner pressure, that sudden surge of water pushing forth only to flow freely, at last, to run unfettered as it must, seeking its own sea. Bursting with passion, the writer bears his well-honed pen, tearing out the underground rusted pipes of hypocrisy and bigotry wherever encountered and squashing the darkness that encumbers all humanity.

"He's a Southerner, my little Billy, you know, a true Virginia gentleman," Elizabeth had said to her friends. "In the end he will be one of us. Mark my words. We can count on the acorn not to fall too far away from the oak tree."

Being a Virginian—the highest recommendation to society that one can possibly have, he thought. His birthright had carried him a long way with friends and acquaintances in the North. Bill smiled to himself. They get a kick out of my genteel Southern background, but I stay in the North now, he thought. I stay far away from the South, as far away as I can. That way I am not reminded of that tremor in my soul. With a sense of irony, he suddenly realized that being a writer from Virginia, now living in the North and working on stories about the South, was an even better recommendation to society.

Yet many of his friends and family and even his doctor had told him he would have to fully embrace his roots if he were to recover from the constant plague of darkness.

CHAPTER 14

Tavern in the Night

In his dreams, Bill was back on stage at Christchurch School and starring in *The Ghost Train*, a British comedy that the headmaster, who had urged Sty to participate, was personally directing. Sty had discovered that year that he felt at home on the stage, playing a part and reciting lines, and the experience cemented him forever firmly in the arts.

Another member of the cast on stage that first winter was a young man by the name of Vincent Canby, who soon became one of Sty's closest friends. Discovering that they had similar interests, the two boys bonded instantly. Sty learned that hardship is always easier to bear when one has a soul mate with whom to share life experiences. From that point on, Sty and Vincent were often seen together around campus.

Vincent, like Sty, had little athletic ability, but unlike Sty, he thought it rather amusing. Few males in the South laughed at such a serious flaw, and Sty resolved to develop the same debonair attitude as his friend. Nonetheless, Headmaster Smith kept after the two boys not to throw in the towel completely on sports.

"It isn't right for you boys to sit around campus after classes reading books or daydreaming," he would say. "You need some exercise. Get over to the gym and shoot some baskets like the rest of the boys."

But the two boys only laughed at the suggestion that free time should be used up in such a monumental waste of energy as endlessly shooting basketballs into some dumb hoop in Marston Gym or running across the soccer field chasing some stupid white ball every afternoon until they dropped on the grass from exhaustion. Not a chance, Mr. Smith.

The day Sty and Vincent discovered the long-defunct school newspaper and decided to start publishing it again destroyed any future hopes for their participation in sports. Their reborn newspaper was no more than a couple of mimeographed sheets of paper stapled together and passed out to the students each month, but the boys took it over as coeditors and threw their combined energy into it. Their early collaboration and natural gift for writing soon made the prep school newspaper sparkle like never before.

The student newspaper was more than a mere outlet for the boys; it became a major source of joy. As soon as classes were over, they would head to their "office," a back corner of the English classroom, and spend the rest of the afternoon writing satire. They mainly poked fun at fellow students, especially the athletes, whom the boys took great pleasure in lampooning relentlessly. That was a first for Christchurch School; but on a somewhat higher plane, the boys also attacked all the flaws and foibles of the faculty and staff with well-aimed darts. The boys relished their creativity and lived for the day-to-day ecstasy of bringing out the next issue.

Maybe Sty had an inkling, as he sat up in bed during the wee hours of the morning, hunched over his flashlight, pen, and writing pad, creating one story after another, that one day he would become a writer. But at that point in his life he was certainly not thinking he would ever become a novelist. Still, at least he was aware of his natural gift for the words that so easily spilled out of his pen and how deliriously happy he was when he was writing. It gave him a feeling of completeness, fulfillment, and contentment that no other activity in life offered.

Vincent also may have been aware that he was headed for a writer's life, but when the men met many years later in life in New York City, neither could recall a point in time when they had specifically talked to one another about pursuing a career in writing.

It was ironic that Christchurch, with its emphasis on athletic prowess, had become the perfect testing ground for the two young writers. Writing was the drug that calmed their restless souls. For Sty, holding a pen in his hand gave him the only relief he could find for the ongoing ache in his heart. Even before graduating, in June of 1942, he became aware that he was not just enjoying his education at Christchurch, but that he actually loved the school. It had become his new home, and it had saved him.

Along with Sty's growing interest in writing came a growing thirst for alcohol. The boys discovered early on that they liked how alcohol made them feel. In those days it was easy to buy beer at local stores; no one bothered to check for ID back then. Or, even better, it could be purloined quite easily from their parents' liquor cabinets. As a last resort, there was also the tavern down the road.

"Hey Sty," Serpent, Poobah, Tom, or Vincent would whisper during English class, or send a clandestine note during study hall. "Let's go down to the dive at Cook's Corner tonight after lights are out."

That was all it took, someone first to suggest the night's caper. Later in the dorm they would go through the motions of retiring for the night, but instead of getting undressed, the three or four pals would lie fully dressed under blankets waiting for lights out and the usual night sounds—muffled snores, lingering coughs, last minute trips to the john, and late whisperings—to wane. When only hoot owls and tree frogs called and sang in the night, the boys knew their time had come.

In total darkness they crept from their beds, headed across the wooden floors for the back door, and descended silently down the fire escape from the third floor to the ground. Like shadows, they crept across the campus, keeping their heads low so they might be mistaken for shrubs in case anyone happened to be looking out a window.

They rounded Bishop Brown Hall and slipped by the chapel that stood like a fortress in the night, guarding the morals of its young student body. They hunched especially low as they passed the headmaster's Southern brick antebellum home, with its six imposing white columns that seemed to glow in the moonlight. They could usually see lights on in the upstairs windows, and

they momentarily stopped to make sure no one was looking out in the night
for any escaping students. The last stretch across campus was the football
field. After braving that open span of green, they moved out to Route 33,
which, by that time, was usually empty of traffic.

The destination was a tavern a mile down the road toward the sleepy
village of Saluda. A colored family owned the small roadside joint, and it
was open every night. Laughing and talking of the day's events, the boys
sauntered down the nearly deserted highway. They always entered the bar
trying their best to look sophisticated, so they might be taken for young men
from Urbanna—or maybe even down the road from Deltaville—out on the
county for a big night. They would take a seat on a stool at the bar with their
money on the counter and order cold beer.

"You boys from Christchurch School?" the owner asked on the first visit.

The boys were stunned that the man would imagine such a ridiculous
idea. Fortunately, Poobah was able to find his voice. "Nah, we're just passing
through town. Bring us some cold beer, please."

The grizzled old man looked the boys over well before he brought them
the iced beer, but they never had trouble getting beer after that first night and
were mainly ignored and allowed to enjoy themselves without any bother. Sty
thought many times afterward that other beers never tasted as good as beer
from the tavern on those stolen nights in Middlesex County.

The boys never talked much, just sat at the bar, drank the beer, and
savored every second of the "grown-up" experience. Sty remembered what
exhilaration he had felt as his eyes slowly adjusted to the dim lights, as he
took in the mesmerizing blink of the red neon sign flashing "OPEN" at the
window, and, finally, with his first swig, the sweet sensation of cold beer
swilling down his throat. He loved going to the tavern and taking in all the
other characters. They never once saw another white man in the place.

Sty enjoyed playing the role of a tough beer drinker, pretending he was
in a Western flick. He would toss back his head, as he had seen cowboys do
when they stood at the bar in some saloon, hold the bottle to his lips, and

take a mighty swig. He then liked to belch and wipe his mouth on the back of his sleeve, in what he imagined to be an uncouth gesture. Sty figured this way the other guys in the joint knew they were really mean, and not to make any trouble.

~⁓

Bill awoke from his reverie with a start. It was late, and he realized he was hungry. The house was quiet, but he remembered there must be food left over from the earlier festivities at the house. He rose silently from his bed so as not to disturb anyone and made his way down the back staircase to the kitchen.

Veala had put the leftover food in the refrigerator, but there was still an array of empty glasses and bottles laid out along the counter. Poor Veala will have all this mess waiting for her in the morning, he thought. He helped himself to a leftover crab cake and ham biscuit. Suddenly aware of a light in the living room, he took his plate and entered the room, munching as he walked. He found his father sitting alone by the fireplace.

"That you, son? They've finally all gone home." His father sat staring abjectly at the Confederate sword that had been his grandfather's, displayed over the fireplace.

"You still up, Pops?" Bill said, leaning over his father's old, slumped, and fragile body and patting him on his shoulder. "Isn't it time you got yourself off to bed?"

Bill sat down to enjoy the cold supper. "Delicious. I sometimes tend to forget just how good this Chesapeake blue crab is."

"You should come home more often, son."

"I was remembering my years at Christchurch School. How we boys would slip out of our dorm and run down to the tavern at Cook's Corner for a bottle of cold beer. Was it good!"

His father chortled. "It made Elizabeth so mad when she heard about those escapades from Headmaster Smith on graduation day!" They laughed together at the thought, like a couple of old thieves who had shared a lifetime of crime secrets together.

"I wonder if that old tavern at Cook's Corner is still there. I think I might swing by Middlesex County in the morning. I'd like to see the old school grounds again before I leave town. I imagine most of it has changed in these last twenty-five years."

"I guess so, son. Nothing stays the same."

After a pause, Bill said, "I suppose I might have tried harder to get along with her."

There was silence, and then finally the last words on the subject. "You did your best, son. Elizabeth did her best, too; you two were poles apart. I guess we all did our best. That's all anybody can do in life. Now let it go, son."

The two men sat again in silence, each in his own thoughts. They could hear the grandfather clock that was once in the stately hallway of Dr. Joseph's home just down the avenue tick-tocking in the foyer. It had a nice hollow sound to the ear, as if it were coming forth from a deep canyon, announcing that all was well in the world.

"She always wanted to become a doctor."

"Who, Pops?"

"Elizabeth. It was her major dream in life, son, but her father did not approve of female doctors. There were mighty few women in medical school in those days, and the few who were certainly weren't Southern women. Old Dr. Joseph flatly refused to send her to medical school along with her brother, Russell. Told her she should become a nurse and take over the nursing school as her mother, Helen, had done. Later, Russell refused to approve her going to medical school, too. Like father, like son. It was a heartbreaking disappointment in her life."

Bill sat in his chair and looked at his hands folded in his lap. He tried to imagine what it must have been like for Elizabeth to have been so frustrated in her life's burning ambition. He could feel some seeds of sympathy stirring within him, an entirely new sensation.

Bill glanced at his father, an old man who looked as tired as Bill felt. "I think it's time to call it a day, Pops. Let me help you upstairs. You must be exhausted."

Later, after his father was settled in his bed for the night and Bill lay in bed in his old back bedroom, his thoughts returned to his youth. He thought about how past events all melt together like ice cubes in a warm dish, causing a man to lose focus on the exact cause of his pain. When exactly did the outrage happen? When was the precise moment of that crushing defeat? His life under Elizabeth now seemed so confusing, a mishmash of angst that he could no longer quite properly categorize.

She is gone, he thought once again. He could be healed at last. He could now return home anytime he wished to the land of his own mother, to Tidewater, Virginia, to the land where he was born and raised, to the land that he loved, to the land that was his by birthright . . . These were his last, jumbled thoughts before his brain mercifully shut down for the night, at long last. He hoped this night he would not dream, and that he would finally enjoy a peaceful night of sleep in his home of yesteryear.

CHAPTER 15

Christmas

Billy, home for his holiday break from Christchurch, awoke with the thought that this was his first Christmas Eve with a stepmother. The realization hit him like an ice pick in the heart. When he went downstairs for breakfast, he was dismayed to see she was already wound up and well into one of her usual morning tirades against him.

"Drinking! Smoking! Staying out late! And look at this disgusting magazine he's brought into our very own home!" With an expression of disgust, she threw a magazine down on the breakfast table.

Billy looked at the magazine in horror. It was one of his favorite girlie magazines, borrowed from a friend at school and smuggled home, where he had wedged it under his mattress. He stared helplessly at the sexy blonde smiling back at him in full living color, her two breasts barely covered by the skimpy top of a hot pink polka dot bathing suit.

"Filth! In my own house! Why, that degenerate boy is lusting for women under our very own roof!" A dark storm cloud of fury raged behind the thin skin of Elizabeth's face.

As if the blonde on the cover had not been enough to hang, draw, and quarter Billy in front of his father, who was seated across from him, Elizabeth thumbed through the magazine to show other lurid pictures. With each glaring photo, Billy felt even surer that his stepmother was right . . . that he was no damned good. As the pages unfolded, the charges were fired like a machine gun lets loose its ammo, the bullets coming at such rapid pace that neither father nor son could find voice to respond. Veala stood in the background rubbing her hands on her apron, her face contorted in anguish. She could do nothing to stop the tirade. Billy sat miserably, staring at a fly that had landed on the windowsill, while his father studied his fork.

Elizabeth paused to take a breath and Veala, as though making a life-or-death decision, bolted from the kitchen with a platter of scrambled eggs and grits and a wide smile on her face. She was humming a Christmas carol. It was not considered proper to have family scenes in front of the help. Veala shot father and son a look of triumph as she ladled out breakfast to the tune of "Joy to the World." She took her time, wanting to make sure the storm had come to a full stop before leaving her charges.

"Now, Elizabeth," Father finally said after Veala had withdrawn to the kitchen, "don't you know, my dear, that boys will be boys? There is nothing in the world to worry about with girlie magazines. Why, every red-blooded American male looks at pictures of half-dressed girls. That's part of growing up, sweetheart. We should be thankful for it."

"Not in my house!" Elizabeth said, in a now controlled voice that had turned icy cold. Her new tone was even more fearsome than her earlier pitch of near hysteria. Both males hunkered deeper into their Windsor chairs, the wooden spokes digging into their backs.

Veala returned with a plate of buttered toast. She took a deep breath, as if she were ready to throw her large body off a cliff and into the sea and needed one last gasp of oxygen. "It's Christmas Eve! The Lord wants us to be filled with love and for everybody to get along!"

Elizabeth turned to glare at Veala, her blue eyes the color of steel. "That will be all, thank you, Veala," she said, dismissing her. Veala, totally defeated, shrugged her generous shoulders and returned to the safety of the kitchen. She had done her best. That was the last they saw of her during the remainder of breakfast, although the diners did hear an inordinate banging of pots and pans as she washed dishes, which Billy assumed was her way of getting in the last word.

Billy took advantage of the interlude to swallow a few more big gulps of food; then, before Elizabeth could restart again, he quickly stood up, excused himself, and headed for the back door. He did not even stop to pick up his winter coat.

"Heathen!" the woman cried as the door slammed, and he was gone for the day. His father cringed at this new word for his son, because he knew the subject of religion also did not bode well with Elizabeth due to Billy's latest and obvious anti-religious phase, but he said nothing, not wishing to unleash another fit from his wife.

It was cold outside under an overcast sky, and Billy spent Christmas Eve shivering inside his light clothing, for he would not return to that woman's house even to pick up his warm coat. The day was long, and he felt as alone as he had ever been in his life amidst the streets of Newport News as they bustled with last-minute shoppers. He imagined the family happiness and laughter he had once known in a home that was filled with a loving mother, holiday aromas of turkey cooking in the oven, plum pudding, pecan pie, popcorn balls gooey with molasses, sweet chocolate peppermint candy, sugared orange slices, and a sparkling Christmas tree surrounded by heaps of merry packages beneath its boughs.

To make things worse, he was hungry. He thought of Veala's delicious hot breakfast, served too many hours ago and which he had not had enough time to complete. He watched the weak December sun slowly make its way across the overcast sky. Finally, when the hands on his wristwatch read five P.M., he went home to crouch behind the shrubs near the garage and wait for his father to return from the shipyard.

There was no sign of life in her house. A light in her upstairs bedroom was on, so Billy decided she was up there reading some ridiculous book on health care. Since it was Christmas Eve, Veala had probably gone home at noon.

Soon his father pulled into the driveway in his old green Pontiac sedan. He looked tired, but when he stepped out of the car and saw his son behind the bushes, a look of surprise came over his face. "Why, Billy, have you been here all day, son?"

The two spoke for a few minutes like coconspirators before entering the house as quietly as possible through the back porch—to no avail. They could hear Elizabeth coming down the front staircase. She was still carrying on about Billy, but the word "heathen" had evolved into "atheist," a far more serious charge, as "heathen" might have applied to someone from a primitive culture not yet blessed by exposure to enlightened religion. On the other hand, "atheist" suggested some bull-headed stepson who had rejected God even after having been properly introduced to Him. It seemed to Billy that the day had not passed and they still were caught at the breakfast table, engaged in the very same bitter conflict.

Billy slipped up the back stairs to wash up for dinner, hoping she would calm down before then. He could hear the ongoing conversation downstairs, his father's soothing words interjected occasionally amongst pauses in her long-winded soliloquies. Finally, his father came up the front stairway and knocked on the door of his room. "Come down for dinner, son."

"I'm not hungry," Billy replied, horrified at what he had just said. After all day on a cold bench with no lunch, he was as hungry as he had ever been in his life. He could have devoured a bear.

"Come on, son. Veala has left a delicious dinner for us. It's Christmas Eve, the holy time. The Christ Child was born on such a night. It's time to put aside our petty squabbles and prepare for the message of the religious season: peace on earth, good will toward men."

It was a quiet dinner, eaten in the formal dining room amongst the portraits of her ancestors, who stared down at the trio. Billy saw himself from a montage of distorted angles reflected in the great quantity of silver vases, goblets, and trays. No one said a word. It was as if she had finally said her piece to her fellow earthlings and now was preparing for the arrival of the baby Lord Jesus. Billy hoped grimly that the boy Jesus would fare better with her than he had.

CHAPTER 16

The Dance

The next morning, Christmas Day, that woman was still in a quiet mode, as if the sanctity of the day had come over her and left her in peace. Still, she adopted a long-suffering look in honor of the occasion, like some early martyr of the church.

After breakfast, Billy took a shower and slicked back his hair with a part on the side to create a more respectable look. He remembered that his mother had always called him handsome and he wondered if that assessment was true. He considered his face for a few seconds in the bathroom mirror, then picked out his best Sunday suit and tie and put them on. After a final inspection in the full-sized mirror on his bedroom door, he knew his mother would have approved.

The entire family was to meet for Christmas dinner at Dr. Joseph's big house not far down Chesapeake Avenue, overlooking the water. Even though the patriarch doctor had passed away earlier that year, the majestic stone mansion where he and his wife had once lived, which looked like a small castle, was still in the estate and would remain so until it was sold. In the meantime, the family enjoyed continuing to gather there for reunions and holidays. It seemed right that they should cling to their culture and traditions as long as was possible.

Billy had no illusions about Christmas with the family. It would be hell—a long, boring day in spite of a smattering of young children. It would be tiresome hearing the family chatter all day long, but it was Christmas, and he held out hopes for some good food at least, and even some Christmas presents at the end of the holiday feast.

They had arrived first so that Elizabeth could speak with Lucy about the food preparation going on in the kitchen. Lucy was Veala's sister and had always come to prepare holiday meals for the family. Soon the rest of the clan arrived. The group sat themselves in the front parlor around a huge stone fireplace that was already lit, blazing and crackling with split oak and southern pine, offering the illusion of much warmth and cheer. Billy noted that even on Christmas, the Buxtons were serious people, very different from his folks. All of the comments concerned the dire and stern: life-and-death issues; each family member's health and various ailments; cleanliness and its role in fighting off ever-present germs. There was never a lot of laughter, fun, or spontaneity. The children, considered to be prospective doctors and surgeons, were treated like little adults and expected to remain silent until someone spoke to them.

The house was still furnished elegantly with antique furniture, oriental rugs, and oil paintings. It reflected the artistic beauty and family values of the past. The caretakers, an old colored couple who had served the family for years and years, lived in the guest cottage at the back of the estate. They had placed the usual Christmas decorations at various points throughout the house: a wreath on the front door, pine boughs gracing the curved front hall staircase, and a Christmas tree decorated with sprigs of red holly berries, dried baby's breath and tiny white lights in the front parlor. Bright packages awaiting their moment to be unwrapped lay stacked under the tree. Things were looking up, Billy thought. He imagined that the long, strange-looking object propped up against the back wall just might be a new fishing rod and reel for him to take back to school and use for fishing in the Rappahannock River.

Billy had met everyone in the family at the wedding, but he realized as he greeted relatives and shook their hands that a few polite words were expected of him. The various siblings looked him over, as if to see whether he was really as bad as their sister had told them. They all looked the same, Billy noticed:

identical thin faces, long noses, high foreheads, pale skin, greying hair. They all looked steeled permanently, like they expected bad news to arrive at any moment.

Helen's new husband, Rufus, stood out from the bunch, with his ruddy, rough-hewn face and stocky body. He was obviously of the working class, not an indoor worker as a carpenter or blacksmith might be, but an outdoor laborer who worked in the fields or woods. He was friendly, and Billy found that he liked him. Billy saw that, like himself, Rufus was also an outsider.

Billy took a quick accounting of the assembled family. Besides himself, Elizabeth, and his father, there were Helen and Rufus; John and Alice, John's "Catholic wife," as Elizabeth always added when she uttered her name. Then there was their son Jack; the perpetually red-nosed Joseph, Jr., a lawyer who worked for the government, and his girlfriend, Lillian, a lovely lady from North Carolina who showed up for family events and was the type known as a "delicate but faded" Southern beauty. The group was rounded out by Dr. Russell and his lovely, redheaded wife, Red, and their two sons, who carried the nicknames Chip and Bucky. The children added a spark of excitement to the group. It was a party of fifteen, and seemed to Billy like a return of the same cast from the wedding day.

The old Dr. Joseph and his wife, Helen, had never touched alcohol, as they had been devout Baptists, but their children, sent to prep schools and fancy universities up North, had quickly picked up more sophisticated habits, which included a taste for whiskey. To a man, their children had become the more socially correct Episcopalians, members of a church far more tolerant of personal habits. A makeshift bar had already been set up off the pantry, just like when the old doctor was still alive, with each adult slyly pulling out a bottle from the innards of a topcoat, and the family was continuing the tradition.

Lucy tended to the turkey, which had been pulled from the oven and was now cooling on the counter. Her usual platters of tomato spoon bread casserole, bourbon sweet potatoes, flaky biscuits two inches high, steaming crab-and-cheese casserole, oyster dressing, mashed potatoes and gravy, Virginia country ham so salty one had to drink a half glass of water after every bite, broccoli-cheese casserole, cranberry and minced orange sauce, and strawberry-banana-cream-cheese congealed salad served on lettuce were lined up across the kitchen in various stages of completion. Billy thought the aroma of such a fine array of Southern cooking was even more glorious than the sight of it.

The kitchen was a busy place, like a train station at rush hour, as the family came in constantly to prepare or refill drinks. They were cheerful in spite of the fact that everyone realized that this would be the family's last Christmas in their parents' old home. Soon after the holidays, the mansion would be put on the market and all the possessions within would be divided amongst the family. Each family member wanted to do his best to keep things festive.

Billy furtively waited for a break when he, too, could slip into the kitchen to make himself a drink. More than one could play this game, he thought. Lucy rolled her eyes at the boy when she saw him lace his cola with a generous measure of his father's bourbon. "You sure do think you're somethin', drinkin' your daddy's bourbon, young man!"

"You won't tell on me, will you, Lucy?" Billy asked, looking up at her with pleading eyes. "After all, it is Christmas, and I'm sixteen now!" Secretly, he did not know how he could get through Christmas dinner without plenty of hard drink.

She shook her big head. "What you do is none of my business, Mister Billy," she said, turning back to whisk the gravy on the stove. "I suspect in time you'll be just like all of them."

"Thanks, Lucy." Billy took a long swig and then quickly poured an extra shot into his drink, just in case he couldn't get back any time soon for a new round.

Lucy shook her head. "Don't think Veala don't notice back at Mrs. Styron's how you lace your lemonade with vodka. That's going to lead to big trouble, Mr. Billy," Lucy added, as if suddenly filled with Christmas spirit, inspiring her to help change the wrongful ways of her fellow man.

"Where is your family today, Lucy?" Billy asked, thinking it wise to change the subject. At any moment, someone could walk into the kitchen, and he didn't want them to hear Lucy admonishing him for his drinking. He suddenly wondered who was fixing Christmas dinner for Lucy's family. His family had never had colored cooks to help them with holiday meals and had always prepared their own feasts.

"Why, they're all home, Mr. Billy, waitin' for me. I'll be fixing them their turkey as soon as I get back home. I got twenty-seven of my family coming for dinner at six o'clock tonight. Now that's a big crowd!"

"Well, Merry Christmas, Lucy," Billy said, lifting his glass to her. He could not imagine anyone having to cook two Christmas dinners in one day. She would suffer from exhaustion, he thought vaguely as he left the kitchen and strolled through the formal dining room, the library, and the front hallway, toward the back of the house. Once he arrived at the back entrance, he stepped out onto the wide porch that overlooked the spacious yard.

A guesthouse stood at the rear of the property with a pond in front of it, trimmed with jagged rocks. He could not resist walking over to have a closer look. Billy gazed down into the cool depths of the water, observing the silent shapes of goldfish moving back and forth like shadows in the deep. Remembering a package of crackers he had stored in his coat pocket in case he got too hungry waiting for Christmas dinner, he tore open the cellophane and let them drop one at a time into the pool. Instantly there was a flurry of bright orange, and then the crackers were gone.

Quickly losing interest in the fish, Billy turned back to the house to continue his investigation. It was fun to have a good look around while the adults chatted. He would go upstairs and search the rooms. Anything was better than sitting around with the family making small talk or answering inane questions about school. He certainly did not want to be roped into having to watch the younger cousins, and he knew very well how parents could so easily draw in older children for this unpleasant task. Then, too, he wanted to dodge any even worse requests for recitations of poetry or a family round of Christmas carols.

He spotted the elegantly curved wooden staircase leading to the second floor and moved silently toward it, hoping no one would hear his stealthy steps on the highly polished but creaky wood. Snatches of conversation from the front parlor followed him up the stairway, laced with a lot of nonsense like "Isn't he cute?" or "He's so big for his age!" probably referring to either Chip or Buck. Billy was glad he had made his escape. He spotted poor Jack reading a book in a chair in the front hall, as far away from the adults as he could manage, and surmised that he, too, was suffering through the holiday.

A long hallway waited at the landing with a pair of twin French doors on one side and a series of six doors that Billy thought probably led to bedrooms on the other. Intrigued, he headed for one of the French doors, which looked the most promising, and flung them open. An enormous dark room awaited him and, as he flicked on the light switches, a grand and princely world beckoned him to enter.

It was a ballroom, Billy soon realized—an ornate and elongated room that must have taken up the entire back half of the second floor of the mansion. The room had highly polished parquet floors and was lined with mirrors with white trim and gilded sconces laced between them. A neat quartet of golden chandeliers, dripping in crystal, hung from the ceiling, emitting sparkling, almost magical light. At the end of the room was a stage where musicians might gather. Dozens of red velvet side chairs lined the sides of the room to accommodate the guests in between dances. It was almost a land of fantasy, a place where no stepmother or other dire problem could ruin a young man's life.

Billy had heard his father speak of the lovely tea dances given at this home. They must have taken place here, he thought. He could envision his father on Elizabeth's arm, and he understood immediately how such a lifestyle could have impressed him and turned his father's head. Billy saw at once, with disgust, that his father had sold out his son for a ballroom.

The image of his father and Elizabeth faded, and he turned to look at himself in the mirrored walls. Instantly, he was standing amongst dozens of beautiful young ladies dressed in pastel chiffon gowns. They were dancing, and their gossamer silken dresses swirled and drifted across the shining ballroom floor. A string quartet of men dressed in tuxedoes played violin and cello. The most melodious music filled the air and spilled out into the hallway, down the stairs, out the front door, and across the bay.

A young girl approached him shyly from the depths of the mirrored reflections. She was dressed solely in white veils that flowed from her body like the soft, rippling fins of fish. He stretched out his arms to her as if he were drowning in the surrounding sea. As the music changed to a Viennese waltz, she fell into his arms, and they danced off into the silvery reflection of mirrors. Billy felt himself swept into a heady gyre of heavenly joy.

Happiness, even if just in dreams, is an exquisite thing, to be deeply appreciated whenever experienced, and forever cherished. But Billy's reverie was brought to a jolting halt. "Well! Look who's here and looking at himself dancing in the mirror!" came the hideous voice. Billy stopped dreaming and stared into the pale blue eyes of his stepmother.

"Dreaming of your little sweetheart?" continued the shrill voice of that woman. Billy saw his beautiful girl and the surrounding sweet violins replaced by the terrifying specter of Elizabeth looming in the mirror's reflection.

She cast cold eyes on the boy through the mirror, and he seemed to shrivel before her gaze. "It's time for dinner," she announced, making the meal sound like an execution. "We are waiting for the honor of your presence before we say our Christmas prayers." She turned abruptly and stormed from the room with Billy meekly following, all the time noticing how her thick heels clicked as she made her descent and how the hideous noise, like the sound of bullets, echoed throughout the entire manor.

He followed her all the way down the stairs into the front hall, through the library, and into the dining room. He saw at once that everyone else had been seated at the elegantly dressed dining room table; they were obviously waiting for him. The room was encased in silence as his father rose to seat his wife next to Dr. Russell. His son slipped miserably into the only other empty seat, at the far end of the table.

"He was up in the ballroom dancing with himself," Elizabeth announced to the group in a voice steeped in disgust. Billy felt shame like he had never known before, a bright red flush sweeping across his face, neck, and body, like flames rushing in the wind across a dry field of hay.

"Now, Elizabeth," his father said. "It's Christmas. The boy has a great imagination. More power to him. Let it be."

"Who will say grace?" asked Dr. Russell from his father's old chair at the head of the table.

"Oh, let Billy say Christmas grace," Elizabeth said, her voice cutting like a knife. "He is our little resident atheist. He should have a nice prayer to share with us on Christmas Day." The horrified group sat silently; no one dared to say a word in the white light of her fury. Dr. Russell kindly saved the day by saying the usual, gentle Episcopalian grace. The excruciating moment was over.

Upon hearing her cue of "Amen," Lucy immediately swept from the kitchen door into the room, filling the table with sumptuous platters of roast turkey and side dishes. Elizabeth's brother John poured wine, and his wife, Alice, was already laughing her slightly shrill laugh. The family, well oiled, began to speak again, determined to have a good time in spite of the tenuous start. Good cheer descended on the group—except for Billy, who ate quietly, overcome with memories of his dead mother at Christmas. His eyes drilled on his plate before him, and he barely tasted the delicious food that Lucy had spent the day preparing. It passed between his lips, went down his throat, and formed a hard mass in his stomach.

Christmas day passed. As the long hours dragged by, Billy realized he had achieved a milestone: the First Christmas. There had been a new fishing rod and reel for him under the tree, just as he had hoped, but somehow the earlier encounter in the ballroom had defiled all the happiness of receiving that long-desired gift. After that shame, he knew with an early premonition of despair that he would never recover, nor ever again have any hope for the existence of a loving and caring God.

CHAPTER 17

Return to Christchurch

Bill awoke at dawn the morning after the funeral with the realization that his dreaded weekend from hell was almost over. He rose abruptly from bed and looked out the window. The sun was just breaking over the horizon, and the splash of so much pink in the sky caused his breath to catch. He slipped on his clothes without even bothering to turn on a light, scribbled a few lines for his father and Rose so they wouldn't worry, and slipped down the back stairway, just as he had done so many times as a boy.

This was the last day that he would spend in his old hometown. He had seen enough of his boyhood haunts to last a lifetime, except for one place: his old prep school in Middlesex County.

Sunday morning on Chesapeake Avenue was usually quiet, and this day was no different. Except for a stray car that passed just as he was pulling out of the driveway, he had the road to himself. The *Daily Press* newspaper delivery boy, bicycling along the sidewalk and throwing out the morning papers, reminded him of his own first job when he had lived in Hilton.

In the wee hours of the night, he had suddenly awakened and known that he had to return to Christchurch, his old school on the Rappahannock River. After crossing the York River Bridge at Gloucester Point, he stopped for coffee and a pair of glazed doughnuts, and after less than an hour spent driving on the empty Route 17, a road that closely followed the same trail that George Washington had once used while traveling on horseback from Williamsburg to Mount Vernon, Bill was back at his old campus once again. Pulling the car up behind the headmaster's home, he turned off the engine, got out of the car, and walked to the center of campus, the site of the old Bell Tower.

The same drop-dead splendor of rural Virginia that he remembered from his days there as a student awaited him: the sweep of rolling green grass, melodic birdsong, distant corn and soybean fields, and blue-ribbon river welcomed him once again. He could see at a glance that the school had grown with the addition of a few more stately red brick buildings since his graduation in 1942. A new athletic complex spread out in the front field, complete with the luxury of real bleachers—something unheard of in his day, suggesting that athletic participation was even more important to students today than it had been in his time.

That certain Sunday-morning feeling at prep school that one almost has to experience in life to fully understand, that overwhelming sensation of loneliness and despair, perhaps merely an ache for one's mother, returned in its usual form of a stab in his chest, just as it had so many times before. Who would want to repeat the years of youth, he thought, when they were so filled with the pain and agony of growing up?

A boy dressed in a sweatshirt and jeans was walking across the grass toward the river. It could have been him on that long-ago first morning at prep school, he thought. He could see himself in that young boy, feel the very same onset of indescribable pain, just as if he had suddenly experienced some mysterious transformation from man to boy. By the way the boy walked, Bill was sure he was new to the school and was feeling the very same feelings he once had experienced himself. Feelings were fully transferable and universal, he realized once again, and they lived on and on through the generations as if they, too, were passed on by genes. Perhaps one day, Bill imagined, scientists would find emotion and ideas every bit as biologically alive as the rest of the animal kingdom.

The headmaster's dog, which had ignored the stranger standing under the Bell Tower, now expertly nosed out of the gate in the picket fence and trotted out on the field to meet the boy. It even looked like the same dog that had once greeted Billy, almost thirty years ago. Could it be? No—he quickly dismissed the thought, but then considered the universality of dogs and their mission, serving the needs of young, lonely boys the world over.

The boy and dog fell in together, walking side by side as if connected by some indivisible thread, and proceeded toward the river. Some things never change, Bill thought, remembering every detail of his own first morning at Christchurch.

With these thoughts moving through his head, Bill turned to the front door of Bishop Brown, which he discovered quite happily was unlocked. He slipped inside and walked up the creaky stairs to his old English classroom. Could its desks be the very same desks he had once used in this classroom? He sat down in one of them to test it, and it certainly felt the same. It looked as if the blackboard was the same, and it surely was the same pencil sharpener on the wall at the end of the room. He could almost hear the whirring sound as boys lined up before a quiz or test to sharpen their pencils for the ordeal, as if sharpening their swords before battle.

He thought of the great writers to whom he had been introduced in this classroom, and their ideas, which had once set fire to his brain, came forth once again like water gushing from a burst main. There were so many he admired. There was Marcel Proust, with his burning sentiment that there was nothing in this world more important than emotion—simple, pure emotion—and his philosophy that a man at the end of his life will not be concerned with how much money he has amassed in some bank, or the fame he has achieved in his life, but solely feast, in those last moments, on the rich feelings he has experienced along the way. Love, joy, happiness, hope, and despair—such innate, primitive, and passionate feelings, experienced over the years, are the best of life. Bill thought it was a shame that most people did not realize this until they were on the verge of death.

And James Joyce, who, as a young man studying to be a priest in Ireland, had gone to the beach one day, only to be mysteriously and profoundly moved by the simple vision of a young woman standing by the sea. The future novelist, the greatest writer of the last century, had seen her hoist her skirt mid-leg and watched, mesmerized by the sight of the waves billowing like lace about her ankles. He had known then, instantly, as he stood helplessly before her, that he had to leave the church and live his life in the pursuit of art. And if he did not do so, he would die. Somehow, Joyce had instinctively known, as had Bill himself just a half-century later, that if he were going to become a writer, he must turn his back on his own people. He must leave Ireland; he must escape all the oppressions of life—the church, his family, his friends, even his own mother—and set out courageously upon new frontiers to pursue total freedom of thought in his journeys with his pen. Bill had not missed the irony that Joyce had subsequently lived the remainder of his life on the Continent, never to return to his beloved Ireland again, but to pour out his passion for Ireland into his books. Bill, too, had left his native land, his emotions seething and ripe, to write of Virginia with a passion so intense that only the furious, estranged, and exiled could possibly wield such a pen.

And there was T. S. Eliot, who had said that a writer's words, once struck on paper and later read, would live on and on forever and be heard again and again within the human brain, transformed into what the great poet had called "flashing fragments"—images so vivid and true to reality they are never forgotten, words so powerful that they ring on and on, like the tolling of some massive bell that passes on from town to town.

Bill thought of how society relied on its writers, in each and every generation, to bring forth universal human feeling and pass it on, often from the dregs of despair. They who do battle with the pen each day deliver nourishment to the human brain, heart, and soul.

All the greats, all the many writers to whom he had first been introduced in this classroom, had given him, as a teenage boy, his first intellectual sense of a world of wonderment, of escape from the unbearable, and the hope of a life truly worth living. For without art, without the written word, without the written idea, thought, or feeling that transcends all the cheap, poor, and ugly, life would be flat, worthless, beyond endurance, a living horror.

He recalled what a nameless woman, one of the many faces he had met at numerous book signings, had once said to him: "I read you because you can tell me what it is that I believe but have never been able to put in words. The thoughts and feelings that you wrote of on page twenty-two in your last book were once swimming in my internal Sargasso Sea. You have discovered them and found words for them and given them to me, and I thank you for it."

As these thoughts came over him, Bill saw clearly how his own message, his modus operandi, his raison d'être had been forged from his father's marriage to Elizabeth, and that she had given him the keen sword with which to write. He now clearly saw that she had given him his working definition of true evil, something every writer must forge for himself. Evil, he had finally understood with every ounce and cell of his person, occurs when a stronger person forces his set of values and rules of life on a weaker person. He also knew that he would have been grossly insincere if he had not dedicated his entire life to the pursuit of stamping out evil as he defined it and wherever he saw it, if he had lived his life as an engineer, or doctor, or lawyer, or whatever she had in mind for him, and never confronted and registered his true feelings in his books and writings.

Bill recalled that when he was twenty-two—near the age of his narrator in *Sophie's Choice*, his present book—and living in New York, he had come down with a truly wretched case of hepatitis. In those days, right after World War II, it was a very serious and unfamiliar disease, and he was sure that he had come close to dying. While recuperating, he had received a letter from Elizabeth. The gist of her letter was that while she was happy that he had recovered, she hoped from her heart that he realized that he had brought the illness on himself, that by the loose and debauched life he had been living, drinking, irregular habits, etc., he had no one to blame but himself for his close call with oblivion.

He was still very weak when he read her words—barely able to get out of bed—and they made, to say the least, a bleak impression on his spirit. In short, he could still say all these years later that it was one of the most hateful and poisonous letters a young man ever received from a vindictive stepmother, and it made him feel like hell.

The memory of that letter was still every bit as wrenching as it had been then; even today he could honestly say he hated Elizabeth for that loathsome, disgusting letter with its terrible freight of puritanical malice. The only reason, as always, that he hadn't written back and told her to go to hell was because of his father and his desire not to make that good man unhappy. How he had lived with her for so long in apparent bliss was a cosmic mystery.

Yet Bill realized that he had "forgiven" her, whatever that meant, for the wounds that she had delivered to him. Until she died, she and his father had visited his family and they'd had some fine times together. He realized that she had displayed sincere affection for all of his children. There had been moments when, in a sort of pitying way, he had possessed warm feelings for her; but, nonetheless, she had been a grim woman, and he was sure that had his father married her, say, five years earlier, when he was just a child, he would have been destroyed. He was amazed to this day that he had allowed himself to have anything to do with her.

Bill turned and left his old classroom of yesteryear. He drove home, bid his father goodbye, helped his wife pack up the car, and drove off to the airport for his flight to New York City. Farewell once more to Tidewater, Virginia, he thought. Who knows if or when I will ever return?

As the airplane lifted into the sky and pointed north, he saw his homeland recede into mere patches of golden and green fields, sewn into a faded quilt laid out beneath him. He had many more places to visit, people to meet, speeches to give, and books to write. He hoped that the funeral weekend and all its sharp memories had somehow cleansed his soul, in the same way that the application of bleach might remove a stain left on damask after a sumptuous holiday feast. Perhaps one day soon he really could forget the "slings and arrows," as the bard had once so well described the many bumps and jolts of life, that had permeated his youth.

As he glanced upward, he saw a phenomenal layer of thick, white, marshmallowy clouds awaiting him. He looked forward to the exciting sensation of becoming engulfed in pure fluff; perhaps, he thought, such fine substance would be as welcoming as heaven, and he would finally be totally removed from the many mundane cares of the world, and he would find some extraordinary relief. Slender sun-laced wisps of mist raced by his window, like smoke at first, just the suggestion of white against blue, and then a creamy white steam engulfed him, with only a hint of fleeting blue in the distance. And then, finally, he was lost in the great white world above.

The stewardess brought him a glass of bourbon on the rocks, and he lay back in his seat in the first-class compartment. He inhaled deeply the fragrance; it was almost as heady and rich as its taste. Now all the pain is behind me, he thought, and only the glory awaits: true bliss, a time of exquisite enjoyment, to dream, to imagine, to recline halfway back, inert in reverie, and embrace the first drink of the day.

Roxbury, Conn.
February 16, 1983

Dear Mary: Your letter was written
with great good spirit and warmth
and I hope I can reply in kind,
at least in part.

Let me begin, though, with a
true reminiscence. When I was
22, the age of the narrator in Sophie's
Choice, and living in New York, I
came down with a truly wretched
case of hepatitis. In those days, right
after World War II, it was a very serious
and unfamiliar disease, and I'm sure
I came as close to dying as I ever
have. While recuperating, I received
a letter from Elizabeth. The gist of
her letter was this: while she was
happy that I had recovered, she hoped
from her heart that I realized that
I had brought the illness on myself,
that by the loose and debauched life
I had been living — drinking, irregular
habits, etc — I had no one to blame but
myself for my close call with oblivion.
I was still very weak when I read
her words, barely able to get out of
bed, and they made — to say the least —
a bleak impression on my spirit. In
short, I can say — some 35 years
later — that it was one of the most
hateful and poisonous letters as

boy of 22 ever received from a
vindictive stepmother, and it made
me feel like hell. Therefore, I really
can't accept your gentle suggestion
that Elizabeth was representative of
stepmothers in general, who are trad-
itionally despised by their 13-year-
old children. I was no longer 13, like
Luke vis à vis Virginia; or your sister's
stepson. I was, rather, a young adult
in full command of my sensibilities, and
I still hate Elizabeth for that loathsome,
disgusting letter with its terrible freight
of puritanical malice. The only reason —
as always — that I didn't write back
and tell her to go fuck herself was
because of my father, and my desire not
to make that good man unhappy. How
he lived with her for so long in apparent bliss is a cosmic mystery.

Of course I "forgave" her — whatever
that means. Until she died, she and my
father visited our family and we had
some five times together. I think she
had sincere affection for all my children. There were moments when in a sort
of pitying way I had warm feelings for
her. But she was a grim woman and
I'm sure that had my father married her
say, five years earlier, when I was
just a child, I would have been destroyed. I'm amazed to this day that I
allowed myself to have anything to
do with her. I rather regret that in

the TV documentary you saw there was more time spent on her than should have been — a disproportionate bulge which I thought was a flaw in the film. And I'm very sorry indeed that Buck was hurt. But I would be insincere now if I didn't register my true feelings.

You're partially right, certainly, about my father's true nature in matters of race. The book version of the old man was considerably idealized and you are correct in seeing that he kept most of the prejudices of his post-bellum Southern generation. But there had been many moments in the past when I had glimpsed in him the sight of a genuine liberal struggling to escape from the flesh of a reactionary (he did in all actuality, as I said in the book, resign as president of the Va. chapter of the Sons of the Revolution when that group endorsed Senator Joe McCarthy) and so I think my portrait wasn't too far off.

I'm glad all is going well with you and Chip. I think of the Tidewater often though it's been many years now since I've visited the Peninsula. Your letter was, at least, filled with good will and an undercurrent of happiness, and I hope that state is always yours.

Thankfully and with love always

P.S. Rose sends her fondest.

Bill

Mary Wakefield Buxton was born in Vermilion, Ohio, attended Randolph-Macon Woman's College, graduated from the College of William and Mary, and earned a master's degree from the George Washington University. She has written a column for the *Southside Sentinel* newspaper in Middlesex County since 1984 and is the author of eleven previous books about love and life in Virginia. This is her first novel. She is the mother of two adult children and lives in Urbanna, Virginia, with her husband, Chip, and her cocker spaniel, Dandy.